THE FIX

As part of the Karachi Police's Counter Terrorism department, Omar Shahid Hamid has survived being ambushed by gangsters, implicated by colleagues in a false case, and, as CID chief, barely escaped the bombing of his office by the Pakistani Taliban. In 2011, following the attack on his offices by the Pakistani Taliban, he took a five-year sabbatical to write books and worked as a political risk consultant. In 2016, Omar returned to active duty as a Counter Terrorism Officer. He has been widely quoted and regularly featured in several publications including *The New York Times*, *USA Today*, *The Wall Street Journal*, *The Times*, *Le Monde*, *Reuters*, CNN and BBC. His first novel, *The Prisoner* (2013), was longlisted for the DSC Prize for South Asian Literature 2015 and is now being adapted for a feature film. His second is *The Spinner's Tale* (2015) won the 2016 Karachi Literature Festival Prize. He received the award again for his third novel *The Party Worker* (2017) at the Karachi Literature Festival in 2018 which is now being adapted for a TV series.

Also by Omar Shahid Hamid

The Prisoner

The Spinner's Tale

The Party Worker

THE FIX

OMAR SHAHID HAMID

PAN

First published 2019 by Pan
an imprint of Pan Macmillan India
a division of Macmillan Publishers India Private Limited
Pan Macmillan India, 707, Kailash Building
26, K. G. Marg, New Delhi – 110 001
www.panmacmillan.co.in

Pan Macmillan, 20 New Wharf Road, London N1 9RR
Basingstoke and Oxford
Associated companies throughout the world
www.panmacmillan.com

ISBN 978-93-89109-01-6

This is a work of fiction. All characters, locations and events are fictitious. Any resemblance to actual events or locales or persons, living or dead, is entirely coincidental.

1 3 5 7 9 8 6 4 2

Typeset by Manmohan Kumar
Printed and bound in India by Gopsons Papers Ltd

To Samar, my true north, my Arya and Sansa rolled into one, my love,
and to all of those fans of an insane game around the world,
who die a little every time the name of this great sport is tarnished
by those who peddle filth through their fixing

CHAPTER 1

Their odyssey will come to an end, one way or the other, here in Kolkata, the city of endless night. It seems somehow fitting, thinks Sanam Khan, as she takes off her helmet to wipe the sweat off her brow, that the journey that she and her teammates embarked upon six months ago, which has taken them halfway round the world, from the well-manicured parks of Australia and New Zealand to the heat and dust of India, will finish here on the banks of Hooghly river, in a city that was seemingly built for epics, in a stadium with the most romantic name in the world. Eden Gardens.

Sanam is once again stunned by the roar of the crowd. The noise of a hundred thousand people, all willing you to fail, is like a physical force, a malevolent spirit that looms over the two young women standing at the centre of the wicket. This is what Babar sir meant, when he said the game changes completely when there is a full house in an arena like Eden Gardens. Having played all of her cricket in empty stadiums and college grounds with unoccupied bleachers, she never understood the significance of a crowd. After all, who in Pakistan ever came to watch women's cricket?

Sanam had always thought that the game was nothing more than a contest of skill. But here, in this bubbling, seething cauldron, the only thing that matters is temperament. Who can absorb the pressure of playing in front of a hundred thousand people? Who can overcome the fatigue, the heat, exhaustion and the nagging anxiety – that feeling in the pit of your stomach that makes you want to puke on the pitch? If Sanam Khan wants to be a champion, she will have to do all of these things.

She taps the crease with her bat and looks around the field. She dares not sneak a look at the scoreboard, because she knows that the knowledge of how far behind they are will paralyse her. And she cannot afford that right now. She is all that stands between a marauding Indian team and victory. And the one thing she has been taught, since she first sat in her father's lap as a 9-year-old to watch a cricket match on TV, is that nothing else matters except defeating the old enemy.

The bowler returns to the top of her mark. It is Vasques, the dark-skinned Keralite. She's perfect, like an automaton: never off her line, ball after ball. It's an effort even to try and work the ball around for a single. As she taps the ball and runs, Sanam feels the pain in her side flare up. It's an injury she's been carrying since Australia. The doctors have told her it's because her petite body frame cannot support the stress of fast bowling. They have advised her to be more careful when bowling, to minimize the pain. The doctors talk as if fast bowling is a disease, like diabetes, something to be managed by being a little more careful in your diet and taking your pills every day. Fast bowling *is* a disease, but of the mind. And Sanam Khan has been afflicted by it from the moment she realized that she could hurl a cricket ball at a pair of stumps 22 yards away, faster than any other girl, or boy, she knew. It's her obsession, her *junoon*, a state of being she can never escape from, no matter how much pain it gives her.

She reaches the non-striker's end and doubles over, clutching at her side and breathing hard. But just as she does, her batting partner, Fatima Shah jogs back to her and shakes her head vigorously.

'Get up Sanam. We are playing India. Never let them see you hurting. Get up!'

Sanam looks at her vice-captain. Fatima is shorter than her, slightly stocky, and in her protective chest gear and pads, topped with a black bandana under her green Pakistan helmet, she looks, bat in hand, like a Roman gladiator. It would be difficult to call the two of them friends because they are very different sorts, but they have certainly been through a lot together. Fatima has served faithfully as Sanam's consigliere these past two years. There have been good times and bad; more bad than good, if truth be told. There have been the insults and taunts and the sheer effort of getting anybody to take the Pakistan ladies' cricket team seriously. Dozens of shouting matches with selectors and board officials who didn't see the point of investing any time or money in a 'girls' team'. And when they finally got somebody willing to play them, there was the terrorist attack on the New Zealand men's team touring Pakistan, which turned the girls, overnight, into sporting refugees, without a home to play in.

For two years, Sanam and Fatima have borne the brunt of everything thrown their way, because they felt that, as the senior members of the team, it was their duty to shield the younger girls from all the bullshit, allowing them to concentrate on their cricket. And slowly, their determination has succeeded. Sometimes in sport, things fall into place and just click for you. And finally, this year, this team of two veterans and a handful of talented but clueless novices, has caught fire.

The signs were evident in their first match in Australia, six months ago. On a green, bouncy track in Melbourne, the sort of wicket that would have normally seen the team bowled out for about 60, the girls went out and refused to be intimidated. Every bouncer, every yorker, every appeal, was met with an aggressive response, an offensive shot, a warning that they would not be cowed by the Australian girls. It had started with Fatima bludgeoning a hundred, but everyone else joined in. The teenager Ayesha Mufti stroked an innings of 75 so effortless, it looked as if she had never played on anything but Melbourne greentops. And then, of course, Sanam herself had blasted the Australians out with her fiery fast bowling. That Melbourne game started a run of 15 victories, ensuring that the girls became the first ever Pakistani team, male or female, to return undefeated from a tour of Australia and New Zealand. That tour was followed by a win in a 'home' series, if it could be called that, played in neutral Sharjah, against the English. And finally, the girl's momentum has driven them here to India, to the Asia Cup final.

It has been a never-ending battle. Even on this tour, after all their recent successes in Australia, the affronts haven't ceased. Sanam remembers their arrival in India, the humiliation of being made to stand apart from the other passengers at the airport, having the sniffer dogs go through their kits while everybody else whizzed past them. And then being hustled out by Black Cat commandos bristling with guns, as if they were some sort of high value terrorists being taken into custody. Being made to sleep in the dressing rooms of Delhi's Feroze Shah Kotla stadium, instead of being put up in a five-star hotel like all the other teams, because the tournament organisers cited 'security threats' and felt it would be safer for the Pakistani girls to sleep and play at the same venue.

As Sanam gets to her feet, the bowler returns to her mark, and begins her rhythmic run up to the wicket. Each body motion is a finely calculated cog in a well-oiled machine. There is an absolute economy of movement in Vasques' bowling action. The ball leaves her hand in exactly the same way that it has so many times. It's like something produced on an assembly line, manufactured to be exactly the same as the one before it. It even pitches not more than six inches from where the previous ball landed; a near-perfect replica. Vasques would be the result if bowlers were produced en masse in Chinese factories.

But cricket is a game of fractions, and Fatima Shah takes advantage of a fractional change in the line, repositioning herself and cutting the ball for four. Betraying no emotion, Vasques turns and walks back to her mark, working on multiple advanced mathematical equations, calculating trajectory and the impact of air pressure on the ball like a supercomputer. Once again, she comes, the action unchanged, and once again she pitches more or less in the same spot. But Fatima Shah is now like a virus, eating through the supercomputer's code. Again, she hops around in her crease, and cuts the ball, slightly finer, for four more. Suddenly, the metronomic Vasques is shaken, almost physically taken aback by Fatima's aggression. Unable to compute what she is doing wrong, she tries to overcompensate with the next ball, changing her line for the first time in her entire spell, aiming for Fatima's toes. Which is exactly what Fatima wants her to do, as she flicks the ball nonchalantly for a third boundary. The hard drive has crashed, the lifeless eyes seem to flutter like a malfunctioning screen, and her captain has to drag Vasques away as she stands staring after the ball like a zombie.

Sanam takes strike for the next over. The Indian captain is the supremely talented Diya Parulekar, and after the damage incurred by the supercomputer, she decides to bowl herself. Parulekar is an icon of the women's game, perhaps the finest batswoman ever. She is also cool as ice, able to absorb pressure with tremendous grace. Parulekar, or DP as she is called, knows the game might be in the balance. India are still ahead, but if the next bowler cracks like Vasques, Fatima and Sanam will bring Pakistan storming through the gates. Sanam's sides feel like they're on fire, but she sets aside all other thoughts, and focuses solely on DP running in with the ball. The first ball is short and sharp, aimed for Sanam's throat. But she backs away and, with both feet in the air, carves it over point for six. The silence of the crowd is so complete that she can actually hear the ball strike the advertising hoarding 100 metres away.

All of a sudden, 20 runs in the last five balls have made the previously unattainable target a bit more attainable. Another three overs, and 30-odd runs to get. DP's next four balls are very reasonable, but Fatima and Sanam are able to milk them for four singles. For the last ball, she tries something different, slowing the pace to tempt Sanam, who is known to have a penchant for the ultimate glory shot, the big left-handed slog over mid-wicket. It's a completely justifiable risk to take, and one that any canny captain would take, especially after posting three fielders on the boundary on the leg side. And, to DP's credit, she suckers Sanam into the shot. It's just unfortunate for her that the ball lands on the steps of the Calcutta High Court, across the street from the stadium.

As Sanam and Fatima meet in the middle of the pitch to bump gloves, both girls see the fire in each other's eyes, and know that the other will not surrender, no matter what. All the insults, all the little snide comments and haughtiness, will be forgotten if they can win here. The two of them are the team's proverbial odd couple. Sanam is the big hitting, fast bowling all-rounder from Karachi with a privileged upbringing, who perfected her cricket in the women's leagues and universities of England. Fatima is the street-smart foul-mouthed batswoman, a coach's daughter who learned her trade while acting as a ball-boy for her father's proteges among the clubs and practice nets that flourished around Lahore's Minto Park. But what they have proved to be expert in, over the past six months, is snatching victories, often from the jaws of defeat. Here in Kolkata, once again, both of them get the familiar feeling. No words have to be spoken between them, but they sense that they just might be about to pull off another great caper.

The best cricketers, like predators, can smell fear in their opponents. And while DP retains her Olympian calm, casually taking her cap back from the umpire, apparently oblivious of the fact that her over has cost India 16 runs, Fatima and Sanam can see the doubt creeping into the expressions of the other ten girls. What was once a sure thing isn't anymore. DP tosses the ball to the off spinner, Sangeeta Sajharaka, but for just half a second, Sangeeta hesitates, betraying her lack of confidence. This is enough for Fatima and Sanam. Fatima pots Sajharaka's first four balls like a snooker champion, placing them perfectly in the gaps in the field. Each ball costs two runs, as both girls, buoyed by the hope of unlikely victory, forget their aches and pains and run their legs off. The equation keeps getting easier. 21 runs needed off the last two overs, becomes 14 off 8 balls. Sajharaka's fifth ball is an absolute peach, the perfect off break, leaving Fatima as clueless as a nun at a porn convention. But crucially, the ball, for all its perfection, doesn't cost Fatima her wicket. At the next ball, Fatima once again restores her dominance over the spinner by coming down the track and hoisting Sajharaka in a perfectly straight arc over her head for four. Ten needed from the last six.

What will Parulekar do now? A conference ensues between DP, her wicketkeeper, Vasques, and Sajharaka. Vasques still looks like she is in a trance, and Sanam and Fatima confer quietly at the other end of the pitch. Surely DP wouldn't give another over to Vasques in her current state. Surely not. But DP has limited options, and so Vasques it is who returns to the top of the bowling mark. Except that the old operating system is now completely gone and a new one hasn't booted up. Vasques' first ball is hopelessly wide down leg side, and the wicketkeeper, despite performing a pirouette worthy of the Bolshoi ballet, cannot stop the ball from carrying to the boundary. Indian heads slump in the field. Even DP betrays a smidgeon of emotion, pursing her lips for an instant. Out of the corner of her eye, Sanam sees a flock of fans wearing blue India shirts starting to leave the stadium. They seem to have accepted that the momentum of the match has shifted irrevocably. At that moment, Sanam decides she is not going to play safe, just tapping the ball around to get five singles in six balls. For her, this match is about more than just winning. It's about making a statement. It's about walking into the lion's den, Eden Gardens filled to the brim with 100,000 people, and beating the old enemy on their own turf, something that the girls' more glamorous male colleagues have never done in a major tournament. This next ball is going to be Sanam Khan's private little middle finger to everyone who has ever doubted her or her team. Even before Vasques has released the ball, Sanam starts advancing down the pitch. She is so far forward that she receives the ball as a waist high full toss. She swings, the connection is good, the sound of wood hitting leather has never been so crisp and the ball travels like an Exocet missile into the top tier of the highest stand. Javed Miandad, step aside, Sanam Khan has finally arrived.

CHAPTER 2

Babar Qadir smiles as he exits the airport. Rehan *bhai* never fails to impress him. Every time he comes to Dubai, Rehan *bhai*, or RB as he is more famously known, asks him what car he wants to be picked up in. He knows of Babar Qadir's fondness for fancy cars. And every time Babar walks out of the Arrivals area, there is a chauffeur waiting to lead him to another exotic vehicle, each one more glamorous than the last. This time, RB had told him he had a special surprise for him, and as he follows the chauffeur into the parking lot, Babar realizes that this one is truly special. A limited-edition Aston Martin DBS.

As he sinks into the plush leather seats, Babar feels a familiar sensation creeping into him: the desire to enjoy wealth. It is a craving that he has been struggling with since he first broke into the Pakistan team as a teenager, all those years ago. It's almost an addiction. His teammates always made fun of his acquisitiveness, but none of them ever realized what it was like to grow up poor. And not the my-father-was-a-government-clerk-and-made-all-sorts-of-sacrifices-so-I-could-play-cricket type poverty, but real poverty. The kind where you're so used to feeling hungry that Babar thought something was wrong with him when, for the first time in his life, at age nineteen, he had a full stomach.

Babar has always said that people who talk about the 'dignity of poverty' don't know the first thing about it. There is no dignity in poverty. It's bad enough being poor under any circumstances, but it's even worse when you're part of a large family, as he was. His family migrated to Karachi from India after the horrors of Partition, having lost everything except the clothes on their backs. Babar was the youngest of seven siblings, and by the time he was born, the family's circumstances could at best be characterized as being extremely modest. His mother, who had been widowed shortly after his birth, at the age of 30, had barely managed to retain half a floor of a chawl in Ranchore Lines. But that meant four rooms, including a kitchen, shared between nine people in the house. That also meant that rent had to be paid every month, or the family risked instant eviction and an uncertain future living on the streets. Food was a distant second in terms of priorities. His mother, a devoutly religious woman who observed strict purdah, could not leave the house to find lucrative employment, so she struggled to make ends meet by hand-stitching quilts from discarded cloth and selling them. In the Qadir household every extra mouth to feed was a liability, unless he or she could start earning or was married off. Babar barely had a childhood. His only memories of it are of playing cricket and feeling hungry.

It was cricket that became their salvation. It wasn't just the only source of recreation, but also quickly became a viable source of income. Yasser, his eldest brother, was a talented wicketkeeper, the best Babar ever saw, and, thanks to his talent, he got a job on a sports basis in a bank. When their mother realized that extra income could be made by her sons by appearing in club and league matches around Karachi, she pushed all of them to take up bat and ball as soon as they were physically able to. Thinking back on it now, Babar reckons he couldn't have been older than 6 or 7, when he first started playing with his brothers as they practiced on the roof of the chawl. The Qadir family matriarch's efforts bore fruit, as all four of her sons managed to eke out a living by playing first class cricket.

Yasser bhai was the one who broke through, winning a place in the Pakistan. But it was Babar who proved to be the hungriest of the brothers. His obsession to escape his poverty made him a more tenacious player, a quality that ultimately led to him replacing his brother as the national team's wicketkeeper. Yasser Qadir managed to retain his place in the Pakistan team for just 13 matches. Babar would be an undisputed regular in the side for over a decade.

His desire to succeed would breed a ruthless streak, that would even condone pushing his brother out of the national side. It was inevitable, he supposes. Both brothers were wicketkeepers playing in the same era, competing ultimately for the same slot in the team. Yasser Qadir was by far the better 'keeper, but he wasn't much of a batsman. And this was the era when one-day matches were becoming more important. That became Babar's advantage. He was a good batsman, and batsmen-keepers were preferred in one-day cricket. Babar started scoring lots of runs in first class matches, till at one point, the press started asking the inevitable question, of which brother was a better selection for the national team. Babar, still a teenager, had youth on his side, whereas Yasser was 15 years older. Finally, the national selectors arranged a trial match for probables in Quetta. Yasser was selected as the keeper for one side, and Babar for the other. But Babar had the inside track. He knew that Yasser had caught the flu and that the cold, dry climate in Quetta would exacerbate his illness. He seized the opportunity, scoring a century and keeping wicket decently enough, while Yasser's affliction debilitated him, and he struggled desperately in the match. Years afterward, long after Yasser bhai had retired from the game, whenever Babar's guilty conscience occasionally surfaced, he would tell himself that he hadn't told the selectors to hold such an important match in Quetta and he hadn't told Yasser bhai to get sick. It had been Babar's fate, his destiny, to make the Pakistan team and if it was at the expense of his elder brother, than that too, was determined by destiny.

But making the Pakistan team did not enable Babar Qadir to realise his ambitions for personal wealth. The Qadir household operated like a Soviet collective, with the matriarch of the house receiving all the money that was earned by any member of the household, and then redistributing it according to her priorities. Babar was unwilling to abide by the same rules that his elder brothers had followed without question. He was a young man who wanted to buy things for himself; watches, clothes, shoes, CD players. And to do that, he had to find a way to supplement his regular income, to keep something for himself. Which is what had led him to Rehan Jumani's door, and into the world of match-fixing.

Yasser bhai had once told him that he had made a bargain with the devil, and such a bargain would only bring him ruin. Yasser bhai obviously said this without the benefit of ever having sat in a limited-edition Aston Martin DBS. True, there had been difficult times in the middle, with the allegations and the inquiries, and the constant abuse of fans who were unforgiving about the match-fixing. But ultimately, Babar had gotten what he always wanted: wealth beyond his wildest imagination. A grand house in Lahore, an apartment here in Dubai, a Mercedes S-class to drive in. Besides, what did Yasser bhai know? He was a mere footnote. He barely played 13 matches for Pakistan and retired as a general manager in his bank, the very picture of boring, middle-class respectability. Rehan *bhai* had taken Babar to places he had never dreamed of going. And if his guess was right about this current summons, he was about do so again.

The thought of more money gives Babar a warm tingly feeling, as the Aston Martin crosses the causeway that leads onto Jumeirah's Palm, driving up the 'Trunk' to the most exclusive parts of the locality, one of the 'fronds' that houses private beach villas. Babar has visited most of Rehan *bhai*'s houses around the world, in Karachi, Delhi, Cape Town, and London, and all of them are stunning, but this one literally takes his breath away. The driver stops in front of the most palatial compound in the street, a mixture between Miami art-deco and old-world Hollywood. An attendant opens the door of the car and leads Babar to the back of the house, where a pool flows from inside the house into a kind of sunken grotto that overlooks the private beach. In the far distance, Babar can see a container ship chugging out to sea from the port. On the other side, the lights of Dubai's skyscrapers become brighter in the dusk, illuminating the city's skyline.

The attendant pulls back a retractable glass panel and ushers Babar into the covered side of the pool. The pool lights give off an ethereal glow as the sun sets over the sea. Inside the covered section, rows of elegant wicker pool chairs recline along the side of the pool. Dimmer lights come on automatically, slowly pushing back the shadows around the water. A sound system softly pipes old Bollywood songs into the room, establishing an old-world ambience. As the brightness of the lights gradually increases, Babar becomes aware of the presence of another person in the pool room. In one corner of the room, a naked man sits uncomfortably on the edge of one of the pool chairs. Babar is surprised when the man offers no greeting, and in fact tries to avoid his gaze altogether. It takes him a minute to realise that the naked man is one of Bollywood's reigning superstars.

'Babar, my boy!' Babar is momentarily startled by Rehan *bhai*'s booming voice. He turns to see a stout, bald man, wearing nothing but a pair of bottle cap glasses and a towel, step out of a pair of doors that connect the pool area to the rest of the house.

'RB! Good to see you!' Babar smiles as RB lumbers towards him, his gait that of a heavyweight boxer, with his broad shoulders and muscular forearms. It's the gait of a streetfighter, a man who dragged himself up from the dregs of society. The paunch on his stomach may symbolise his current respectability and prosperity, but Rehan *bhai* doesn't allow anyone to suffer any illusions that he has forgotten that he came from the streets.

RB envelopes Babar in a hug that makes the younger man feel as if his ribs are being crushed.

'Did you enjoy the car? Do you know, its fucking James Bond's car!'

'It was magnificent RB. Was it really the one they used in the movies? Couldn't be?'

'Same model. Same colour. I told you I'd send you something special this time!'

'Is it yours?'

'I'm testing it out. One of this fucker's friends', RB points at the naked Bollywood star, 'owes me about half a mil. But he's a bit cash strapped right now, so he sent me the car, in lieu of his debts. I'm considering accepting his offer.'

RB turns toward the naked movie star, who finally makes an attempt to cover his genitals with a towel. 'And since I'm feeling so fucking generous, here's something for you. I shouldn't give it to you, after all the attitude you've shown me in your last couple of projects.' He throws a paper parcel at the naked man's head.

The man doesn't seem to mind, and opens the parcel and starts counting what look to be wads of dollar bills to Babar. He looks up at RB, who now towers above him, and asks, in a meek voice, 'How much is it?'

'That depends on you. How much do you think your ass is worth?'

The man stares at RB, as if trying to actually calculate a dollar value for that question. It only seems to occur to him after a minute or so that the question was rhetorical. So, glancing cautiously towards Babar, and trying to clutch the parcel and keep the small towel in place over his genitals, the Bollywood star finally rises from the pool chair. 'Can I go and wash up now? Please? Your…stuff…it's dripping out of my…butt.'

RB grunts his approval. 'You fucker, you think you're the biggest fucking box office star in India, so you're above it all? You think only the poor starlets have to suck cock? I don't give a fuck who you are, in RB's house, everybody who comes here, man or woman, sucks my cock. Now get the fuck out of here and remember, you're giving me twenty percent of the cut of your next live tour, got it?'

The movie star nods vigorously, willing to agree to anything at this moment, as long as RB lets him go. He then slinks past Babar and RB towards the double doors of the house. Babar gives RB a quizzical glance.

'Saala, fucking big shots. Always trying to put one over me. That's why it's good, once in a while, to teach these fuckers a lesson. Outside this compound, he thinks he's God's gift to mankind. He came here to ask me for a huge fucking favour, to put up 40 crores for his next film, and acted as if he was doing *me* the favour. That's why I decided I'm going to fuck him in the ass today, even though I wasn't even particularly turned on by him. And god, he smells worse than my cook! He gets paid a million dollars a year to hawk some fucking brand of cologne, you'd think he might use some of it on himself once in a while.'

'That's not why you called me here, was it?'

'No Babar, you're too fucking ugly. I only fuck movie stars.'

Both men laugh uproariously at the joke, but Babar's laughter is perhaps tinged with a smidgen of relief. An attendant walks in, carrying drinks and a newspaper on a tray.

Babar sighs as he sips the perfectly mixed Gin and Tonic and raises his glass.

'You think of everything RB. You remembered. My favourite drink.'

'How could I forget? Remember that club in Manchester, when you insisted that I buy that 2000-pound bottle of some fucking premium gin that nobody had ever heard of? And that lasted us, like, an hour, barely? Cheers.'

RB hands Babar the newspaper from the tray. It's a South African paper, *The Daily Sun*. 'The South African president has been accused by yet another girl of rape. So what? What does this have to do with us?'

'Page two. Look at the picture. See anybody you recognize?'

Babar opens the paper and looks at the picture of an unconscious man being wheeled out onto an ambulance by paramedics. 'Wait. Isn't that…'

'Hanif KitKat. Yes.'

'But he was your man in Jo'burg, no?'

'Was. Till the fucker got greedy. Went out on his own. Started talking to the South African boys about setting up a separate fixing pipeline.'

'But the story says he died of a heart attack?'

'Cocktail of Beta blockers and cocaine. The boys had to force a lot of cocaine into him, but it worked. Looked like an overdose. And the local police knew KitKat by reputation, so it came as no surprise.'

'The boys…gave him the cocaine…'

'I couldn't let it go Babar. He cost me five million dollars on the India-South Africa series. That kind of thing isn't good for discipline.'

'But…I've met him…several times. In fact, every time we toured South Africa. He even had my phone number…what if the police start investigating…'

'They won't. Trust me. Read the story. It says it was reported as an overdose case. No implication of foul play. My sources in the South African police say the file has been closed. Don't worry, I sent Saleem Euro to handle everything personally.'

'Ok. So why did you call me? You said there might be some opportunities?'

RB pauses as the music system starts playing *Yeh Kahan Aa Gaye Hum* from the movie *Silsila*. 'Listen to this song. It's my favourite. Lata Mangeshkar at her absolute peak.' He starts humming the lyrics as the song plays, oblivious of having left the conversation incomplete. He listens intently for a full five minutes, until the song finishes. 'I called you for something else. This Women's Asia Cup. It was fantastic. For the first time, the punters showed a heavy interest in women's cricket. There was over thirty million dollars' worth of betting on this tournament. I reckon that figure might treble with this women's World Cup, now that the punters have realized that this too, is a sport.'

'Wow. That's big money RB.'

'Yes. And to the best of my knowledge, I'm the only one who has the inside track in the women's game. And apparently, the hottest property in the game are your girls. The pundits are saying they are one of the favourites for the T20 World Cup in England this summer. So tell me, are they virgins? Fixing wise?'

RB chuckles at his joke, while Babar takes another sip from his gin and tonic and considers the question.

'I think so. I mean I'm pretty sure. They're totally clean.'

'And there wasn't any hanky-panky from their side in this Asia Cup?'

'No. Why, did you hear about anything?'

'No I didn't. Just making sure that they hadn't been approached by any other syndicate.'

'If someone had approached the girls, I would have known. Sanam, the captain, is very close to me.'

'Excellent. Well, Babar, the time has come for us to make money together again. I want you to use your relationship with the girls and introduce them to Saleem. Encourage them to do business with him. I'll also put another couple of plans in play. But it's imperative that you hook them up with Euro.'

'What if they don't go for it? They're pretty independent-minded RB. It's not like the old days.'

RB picks up a thick envelope off the tray and hands it to Babar. 'That's exactly why I pay you the big bucks Babar. To ensure delivery of services. To *convince* them of the merit of our arguments. There are other ways to convince them as well. More *intensive* methods. But I'm sure you won't let it come to that. You have an incentive not to. Here, consider this your retainer. There'll be a lot more of that if we can fix the World Cup.'

Babar Qadir stares long and hard at the envelope bursting at the seams with notes. Once again, there is a choice to be made in his life. But the longer he stares at the envelope, he knows that this is really no choice at all.

CHAPTER 3

The first inkling Sanam gets that her life may have changed in a very radical way, occurs a week after the team's return from India. Having spent most of that time sleeping and recuperating from her injuries at home, one morning she is shocked to find Shamim, her maid, carry in a sack filled with mail into her room.

'*Baji*, this is from the postman. He says they have two more sacks, as full as this one, lying in the post office, but he couldn't carry them on his cycle. You need to send the car over to pick up the remaining mail.'

'But why are we getting so much mail?'

'We aren't *Baji*. You are. They are all fan letters and marriage proposals. And this is all in the last week, since the Asia Cup win. Also, your mother is asking you to come down and sort out the mob gathered outside the house. They're all young men wanting to meet you. One of them claims to have carved your name on his wrist. I didn't believe him though. I told him he didn't look like he could carve an aubergine, leave alone your name on his wrist. Duffer.'

Sanam smiles at Shamim's irreverent tone and stares disbelievingly at the pile of mail at her feet. Then she walks to her bedroom window balcony, which overlooks the house's sprawling lawn. This has always been her favourite spot. As a schoolgirl, she used to gaze out from this balcony every morning, surveying the perfectly cut lush grass and imagining it to be Lord's, or the Oval. As she looks out from the balcony today, she looks past the lawn and the expansive driveway filled with half a dozen cars, to the front gate. Shamim wasn't lying. There is a crowd of people gathered there. They are mostly young men, several of them holding up posters of Sanam. All of this is scarcely believable for her. Sure, she has been the Pakistan women's captain for two years now, and a leading player in the team for almost ten, but she has never gotten this kind of adulation. Women's cricket was never on the radar for most people. Sanam remembers accompanying her parents to innumerable family dinners for years, and, upon telling some old aunt or uncle that she played cricket, hearing the startled response that they didn't realize there was such a thing as a Pakistan women's cricket team.

'Well, are you going to do something about the hordes at the gate or do I need to call uncle Mushtaq and ask him to send some of his policemen?' Mrs. Khan is the matriarch of the household, and she looks every inch the part. Her hair is well coiffed, with new blonde streaks designed to make her look younger than her 60 years. She always wears the most elegant clothes, her kurtas delivered to her at home by the top designers in the city in advance of the public release of their collections. Her signature diamond earrings are understated but unquestionably and obviously expensive. And the tone of her voice is always commanding, as befits a woman who has, over the best part of 30 years, become accustomed to dominating people, whether it is the servants in her house, the board members of the various charities she has championed, or indeed, her husband. In fact, the only person that Mrs. Khan has not been able to browbeat is her eldest daughter.

That fact is a constant source of aggravation to Mrs. Khan. It was never her idea to allow Sanam to play cricket, much less choose it as a career. Mrs. Khan believes that all good things in life are achieved through careful planning and preparation. Thus, in the last three decades she has, like a supremely meticulous general, planned her family's every move strategically, from her husband's investments, to her own selection of which charities to support, to her plans for when and to whom she would like to wed her three daughters. Her husband has always marvelled at her almost Prussian efficiency, and sometimes jokes (but never too loudly, lest she hear), that if his wife had been one of Hitler's generals, we would all have been speaking German today.

But for all of Mrs. Khan's successful stratagems, Sanam's passion for cricket has always defeated her. She could never stop her husband from transferring his love of the game to their eldest daughter. Nor, despite several attempts, could she quite dissuade either father or daughter from taking this obsession from the TV couch into the playing field. Like a guerrilla insurgency, before she had even understood fully what she was up against, father and daughter had snuck through her defences.

And so Mrs. Khan decided to wait it out. She figured Sanam would have to outgrow it sooner or later. She contented herself with the belief that as her daughter grew into her teenage years, there would be other distractions; boys, clothes, the desire to 'be cool'. When that failed, Mrs. Khan was sure that when Sanam went abroad for university, the enormity of the experience would dull the cricketing instinct. In fact, the opposite occurred, as Sanam selected her universities based on which ones had the best cricket coaching programs. Finally, Mrs. Khan had clung to the hope that playing for three years in university and in semi-professional leagues in England had exorcised the demon within her daughter's soul. After all, it wasn't like they had women's teams here in Pakistan. Besides, according to Mrs. Khan's plans, her daughter was supposed to return home from university and work for a few years in the swanky air-conditioned office of some foreign bank or multinational, and then get married to some perfect gem of a *rishta* that she had devised, perhaps a New York based investment banker, or the sole heir to a textile fortune. If Sanam felt really bolshie, she might continue working till the couple decided to have children. But playing cricket, like travelling to Mars, was just not an option that existed in Mrs. Khan's world. Unfortunately for her, Sanam's return home coincided with the cricket board's first efforts to establish the women's game, and Sanam became the perfect fit in a fledgling team due to her experience of having played professionally in England.

Over the years, Mrs. Khan's efforts have been hamstrung by the fifth columnist in the family, her husband. Mr. Khan's encouragement and nurturing of his eldest daughter's passion for cricket is the one act of defiance he has committed against his wife in their 37 years of marriage. Gulrez Khan has been a cricket tragic all his life. He reluctantly took over his father's tobacco business 30 years ago for two reasons. His family assured him that the work was so streamlined and the profits so certain in cigarette manufacturing, that he could devote all his time to watching cricket; and his new bride, worried that her husband was about to throw away his inheritance over this silly game, hinted that tobacco advertising could get him more closely involved in cricket. The plan worked, Khan cigarettes kept selling themselves with little or no assistance from Gulrez Khan. With the family's future secured, Mrs. Khan could throw herself into the work of fundraising for cancer charities, while Mr. Khan could become a proper cricket groupie, often travelling to see the Pakistan team play in Sharjah, or England and even in Australia.

After she bore her first two daughters, Mrs. Khan often wondered guiltily if her husband ever felt bitter about the absence of a son. He would dearly have loved a boy to play cricket with. But Sanam had more than made up for that absence by fulfilling Mr. Khan's every vicarious dream. When she made her debut, she came home and gave her first Pakistan cap to Gulrez. It is among his proudest possessions, kept in a glass case in his study, and occasionally taken out when he goes for golf with his friends, where he always finds an opportunity to mention the fact that he is the father of a Pakistan captain.

'Oh Maa. They're hardly hordes. There aren't more than ten people out there. They'll go away in a bit.'

'I don't care if they're ten or ten thousand. They're blocking the gate. It's all fine for you, sleeping all day, recovering from your injuries, but some of us have to run chores around this house, and it's very inconvenient to find yourself under siege from eight in the morning. So can you please go downstairs and show them your face for five seconds so that we can get rid of them? And can you please change into some proper clothes? It would be nice to see you wearing something without an athletics company's logo. And have you heard of a modern invention called a blow dry? Or make up? Honestly, sometimes I think there's no difference between you and Shamim.'

Sanam stretches and sneaks a look at the floor-length mirror in her room, as she ties her shoulder length-hair with a rubber band. She is pleased with what she sees. She has always known she was attractive, as evidenced by the legions of boys who constantly wanted to date her in school and in college. She has a pleasant face, but it's her eyes, grey-green and stormy, that men find truly bewitching. And years of gruelling physical training have given her, except for her broad fast bowler's shoulders, a lithe, slim and extremely feminine body. Her aversion to makeup has been a long running battle between her mother and her. She never wanted to look or dress like her mother's friends' Barbie-doll daughters, with inches of foundation on their face and nothing but comments about the latest designer *lehnga*s on their lips.

She ignores her mother's comments and nods towards the pile of mail lying on the floor. 'Shamim says a bunch of the letters in there are marriage proposals. Things are getting a bit crazy.'

Mrs. Khan rolls her eyes. 'Well, you might as well have a look at them. Considering you've rejected every single proposal I've brought to you in the past ten years, maybe we should try a more novel approach. Maybe we can get a TV channel to make a reality show out of it: Who will marry the cricket captain? That might be my only chance to get grandchildren.'

Sanam pulls a face at her mother. 'Oh Maa, for once, it would be nice if you stopped with the drama. Sabeen's getting married, isn't she? She seems to like the fellow, and he looks normal. Normal enough to procreate at any rate. There you go, that's your grandchildren right there. You should be happy.'

'Happy? Happy that my two younger daughters will both get married before my eldest daughter? Happy that you can't even attend Sabeen's engagement because you're playing a silly World Cup? How can you miss your sister's engagement? What will her in-laws think? How am I supposed to introduce you to any boys if you're not even present at the function?'

'Maa, come on, we've been through this. It's the World Cup. I can't not go to the World Cup. We've got a chance to win it. We're going in as one of the favourites. I will never do anything more meaningful in my life ever again. At best, I've got one more World Cup in me, but we'll never have as good a chance to win as this year.'

'Another World Cup? You're going to be 31 this year Sanam. You'll be 35 by the time the next World Cup rolls around. Who will want to marry a 35-year-old ex-cricketer? This is not England, or Australia. You are a Pakistani girl. Never forget that. You have duties and responsibilities to your family. You can't play cricket the rest of your life. When will you grow up Sanam?'

'Maa, I'm not having this conversation again. I'm sorry I'm not your picture-perfect daughter. But this is my life. This is my job. I play for my country, and nothing is more important to me than that. Baba Jan understands. He always has. I don't know why you can't.'

Mrs. Khan shrugs her shoulders and turns to leave the room. 'I hope that one day, when you and your father wake up from this little fantasy of yours, it isn't too late.'

*

Fatima Shah is also realizing that her life has changed after the Asia Cup win. It's still early, barely eight in the morning, by the time she finishes her practice session. Construction workers are just replacing the panaflex panel on the giant billboard that towers over the Minto Park nets, and is clearly visible from the new Bypass, as well as all the way to the Lahore Fort. The smiling visage of Bollywood's reigning power couple hawking shampoo is being taken down and replaced with a massive panel of Fatima and Sanam, sharing a Pepsi. Fatima has to shield her eyes to stare up at it, and she is struck by its size. Her teeth in the panel, prominently on display in a wide grin, are taller than she is. It also makes her a bit self-conscious. She never realized her teeth were so big, and she instinctively covers her mouth as the young bowler who has been bowling to her for the past hour, approaches her with a piece of paper in his hand.

'Oye, what are you staring at *kanjar*? What is this piece of paper, your fucking phone number?' This is Fatima's natural reaction to boys approaching her. She has learned to be aggressively brusque. She has always had to be this way, dealing with scores of teenage boys as she helped her father run his coaching clinic for years. There was no place for being meek, growing up around young men who thought they were God's gift to humanity.

'No *baji*, nothing like that. I just wanted your autograph. That's why I came in so early. I wanted to be able to tell everyone in my neighbourhood that I had the honour of bowling to you.' Rivulets of sweat pour down the boy's face. He is a young fast bowler, and she has made him bowl at full pace for the past two hours, to test herself. He has done it without respite and without complaint, just so he could get her signature. Fatima looks at him as she signs the paper. There is no sense of exhaustion, only joy on his part, as if the autograph makes up for all his efforts in the past two hours. She cannot help but feel a little stunned.

Fatima has always enjoyed practicing early in the morning. In Lahore's long summers, starting almost immediately after Fajr prayers enabled her to escape the debilitating heat that envelopes the city from April to November. Besides, early morning was the only time she could ever get a chance to bat. The afternoons and evenings at her father's net coaching sessions were always reserved for the boys. She would be there as a silent spectator, taking in all the tips that her father imparted to the boys, picking up pieces of kit, chasing after balls and, if she was really lucky, occasionally getting a chance to bowl her off spinners in the last half hour, when the regular bowlers had exhausted themselves. That's why she learnt wicketkeeping. Someone had to don the gloves to help out with fielding sessions. Plus, the spare bowlers, who were trying to get their line and length right before going into the net, needed someone to bowl at.

Every day, she would watch the batsmen in the nets, desperately itching to have a go herself, to try out the techniques that she had seen her father teach the others, but she never got a turn. She always had to wait till the morning. It was a struggle getting bowlers to bowl to her. She often had to resort to bribing the younger boys, who hadn't gotten enough time in the nets, with the promise of putting in a good word for them with the coach, and buying them bottles of Coke as a reward for their bowling sessions. Fatima payed for a lot of Coke bottles as she grew up. But after a while, the bowlers didn't mind showing up early anymore. They started to understand that bowling to her improved their own game. The rumours spread about the perfect batting technique that the coach's daughter had and how it was impossible to get through her defences. Soon, some of the older boys also started showing up for these morning sessions, to test themselves against this Supergirl. She would challenge them to get her out, and that's where her investment in Cola drinks started paying off. More often than not, at the end of a morning session, it was now the boys buying her Cokes or a *halwa puri* breakfast from the Old City nearby.

She packs up her kit and starts to walk the route that she has walked every day to go home. Today though, as a further indication of her newfound celebrity, the starstruck fast bowler runs after her and offers to carry her kit for her. Home is not far, and if it weren't for the detour she now has to take because of the new highway, she would literally only have to cross the road to get to Shahdara. It's one of the lower income parts of the city, not quite a slum, but never really able to rise out of its desperate circumstances. They say Shahdara has been like that since the time of the Mughal emperors. A rough neighbourhood filled with rough people. Even more reason why Fatima couldn't afford to be meek, growing up. The meek don't last long in Shahdara.

But Shahdara takes genuine pride in the fact that one of theirs has 'made it'. Smaller posters of Fatima, similar to the mega-panel overlooking the highway, are plastered on almost every wall and street corner. As she walks home, many of the neighbourhood's patrons acknowledge her with deference and respect, and ask after her form and fitness. In a way that she could never imagine, women's cricket has really caught on. Perhaps it has to do with the serially inept performances of the men's team, who haven't looked like they could win anything since that famous World Cup, twenty years ago. Maybe people just got tired of watching losers. Or perhaps it has to do with the fact that, with unemployment rising in Shahdara, people have nothing else to do but watch any kind of cricket they can on their mostly illegal cable TV connections. Whatever the reason for the sudden interest in women's cricket, what is clear is that Shahdara loves its most famous daughter.

Her father is one of the oldest and most respected coaches in the area, but that has never translated into significant material benefits for the family. They have lived in the same cramped, three-bedroom house since before Fatima was born. It's a house that dates back to pre-Partition days, one of the oldest in the locality, and it looks as if it will fall apart at any minute. Only now, thanks to her recent success, has Fatima been able to fund some basic renovations, a proper kitchen for her mother, and a separate room for herself on the roof, finally allowing her the luxury of not having to share a bed with her sisters. Fingers crossed, she hopes that if the team has a successful World Cup, she will be able to perhaps finally move the family out to Johar Town, one of the city's respectably middle-class neighbourhoods.

Her father never had the money for them to move elsewhere. For as long as she can remember, she has seen her parents living month to month, struggling to make ends meet. Fatima can count on the fingers of one hand, the number of times she or her sisters have worn brand new clothes. There was never money for any frivolity or any kind of fun. Any savings that her father had were always spent on his boys. He always regarded his protégés as his real family. If a bright prospect needed new kit, or needed to be transported to distant venues for matches, or needed to be fed, Shahji would fund all of these expenses from his own pocket. He was always ready to spend his last rupee on his boys; never on his own family.

Her father's obsession with his boys has been the centrepiece of Fatima's life. They have meant everything to him, his sense of his own worth judged by their successes and failures. Pushing them harder and harder to become better players, acting as a father to them, while being more or less absent in the lives of his own children. It was perhaps fitting, she thinks, that the Almighty did not bless him with a son, until just six years ago. Fatima can only imagine how her father would have pushed a son of his own. Even now, she sees him watching her baby brother, pacing like an impatient predator, waiting for the day the boy can grip a full-size cricket bat, itching to start on him. Shahji has always believed that he had it in him to produce a Pakistan international. In 30 years he hasn't succeeded yet. He's come close a few times, with dozens of his charges having played First Class cricket, and several of them even having reached the fringes of selection to the National team. But no one has quite managed to break through that glass ceiling yet. Shahji has often said that if only he could impart his coaching knowledge to someone with his own DNA imprint, he could finally break through and produce a great Pakistan cricketer. The irony is that he is not wrong. His genes, coupled with his coaching, have actually produced one of the finest players ever to wear the green cap. But for Faqir Shah, it doesn't really count because it's only his eldest daughter.

CHAPTER 4

The trophy room of the national cricket board is a place for sober reflection. It is a place where a nation's pride, the accrued glory of seven decades of cricketing accomplishment has been piled up together, like bullion in a bank vault. Every cup and trophy in this room has a story behind it, an epic contest fought in some distant land, an inspiring tale of a victory secured, either due to the emergence of a young champion with nerves of steel, or perhaps the coming together of wise old heads overturning the advances of age and delivering one last time for their country. Unfortunately, in recent years the trophy room has become a melancholy place. Those deposits of glory have been shrinking, the stories growing older and older, unreplenished by newer tales. The national team hasn't added new trophies to this room for years.

It was this depressing fact that made Babar Qadir shift the trophies out of the basement of the stadium to his office suite, perched high above the stands and overlooking the pitch of the Gaddafi stadium. As a member of the golden era of Pakistan cricket, he helped to lift many of the cups that adorned the trophy room. He lived through the years of glory, and he wanted to give the modern generation of players a feel of that glorious past. He figured that, by at least looking at the trophies in his office, somebody out of the numerous players that visited him daily, would occasionally look at the trophies and hopefully gain some inspiration. Sadly, the strategy hasn't worked, and his four-year tenure as the cricket board's secretary has seen successive failures on the field. Until now.

The success of the women's team has taken just about everybody who has anything to do with running the game, by total surprise. Which just goes to show exactly how plugged in the cricket board has been about the state of women's cricket. The only one who hasn't been surprised, is Babar. He was the first one to see the potential in this team. Or, more accurately, the potential in the team's leader.

He still remembers the first time he saw her. It was soon after his retirement. The ignominious nature of his exit, hounded by the match-fixing inquiry, had ensured that he was unlikely to be considered for any of the plum coaching jobs around the men's team. The only job he was able to secure in fact, was the lowly position of coach of the women's team that had only just come into being. The board had set up trials to find recruits for the team, but the trials were unlike any trials that Babar had ever attended before. The concept of a women's team was treated as a joke by the board. As an indicator of the low value the board put on the team, the trials had been scheduled not at the National Stadium in Karachi, which was the Board's premier international sporting complex, but at the tiny Deaf and Dumb Association ground, tucked away next to the sea. The ground's facilities were so sparse that they didn't even include a changing room, so that the girls who showed up had to play in whatever they had come wearing.

On top of the board's desire to treat the women's team as comic relief, it also seemed to Babar that many of the aspirants who showed up to get selected were equally keen to play the role of jesters. Some of the girls just started bowling in their shalwar kameez and sandals, some didn't even know how to grip a bat, and a few confessed that they had only showed up because they thought there was a chance some of the male players might be around. There was only a small core of girls who seemed serious about the game. And Sanam had been the best of the lot by a country mile. She didn't really mingle with any of the others, but Babar saw in her that day, and every day since, a hunger to succeed. She bowled for almost two hours in stifling heat, where none of the other girls could do more than 20 minutes on the trot. And the consistency of her pace and line was unchanged from first ball to last. Babar felt sorry for her having to bowl for so long to some of the others who were so inferior to her in terms of skill. So he decided to put on a pair of pads and jumped into the net himself, to assess her personally. Her first ball to him was aimed at his forehead, forcing him to duck and weave as if he were facing one of the great West Indian fast bowlers. There wasn't a hint of deference in her. She had what Skipper used to call 'Fire in the belly.' Babar liked that, and knew then, that she was the first name he wanted on a team sheet.

Some years later, it was Babar again who pushed for Sanam to be made captain of the team. She had never been considered for the job before because she had never lobbied or politicked for it, unlike many of the other girls. The other selectors, each of whom had their own candidate, acknowledged her abilities as a player, but weren't convinced of her potential as a leader. They said she was too aloof, because of her relatively privileged background, and they didn't feel a 'Burger *bachi*' would be able to lead the team. But Babar saw that the fire that burned within her, the hunger to win, would make her the leader the team needed. It was the same hunger he had recognized in himself as he struggled and fought his way to becoming Pakistan's most accomplished wicketkeeper, despite the fact that his greatest rival was his own elder brother. And so he had argued long and hard with his selectorial colleagues, and finally managed to get his way, not because he had managed to win them over, but more due to the fact that all the other candidates hated each other so much, that Sanam became the compromise choice everyone was willing to accept.

Now of course, it's become fashionable around the board offices to take credit for spotting the potential of the girls' team. Especially after the Asia Cup win. Whenever he hears his colleagues go on about how and where they 'discovered' Sanam, he laughs. The men who run this board don't have a clue. They are either government appointed bureaucrats, looking for a comfortable sinecure in lieu of a powerful posting in Islamabad, or retired players like himself, desperate to cling on to the gravy train of lavish daily allowances, first class travel, and the reflected glow of the most valuable commodity in Pakistani sport, the cricket team.

Admittedly, the men's team has been disastrous over the past decade. At any given time there are more cliques within the team than in the Chinese Politburo, each promoting its own candidates for captaincy and playing slots. In the last half dozen years, Pakistan's male cricketers have abused each other on the field, physically assaulted each other off it, sued each other in court, and in at least one case, allegedly conspired to kill each other by hiring underworld hitmen. And this is not to mention their myriad associated problems, such as drugs, hookers, statutory rape charges on foreign tours, and of, course, the small matter of being incapable of winning a cricket match. But despite their lack of success, they have continued to be revered as gods by a majority of the 200 million entertainment starved citizens of this country.

But the success of Sanam's team has changed all of this. The public, having walked for years in an endless desert of failure, has suddenly found an oasis of success. Suddenly, the Girls in Green, as the popular press has named them, are the cricket board's hottest commodity. Rehan *bhai* and the Syndicate's interest in them is the ultimate proof of this.

'Ah girls, come on in. On time as usual.'

Sanam and Fatima walk in, still wearing their practice gear, their foreheads glistening with sweat from their just concluded net session. Babar can see the practice nets from his window, and he knows that so great is the girls' desire for his approval that they have not wasted a minute in reaching his office after their session. As always, their eyes wander towards the trophies in the room. Babar smiles indulgently and allows them a moment to reflect, while a peon serves tea and biscuits. This is not the first time the girls have seen the trophies, but every time they come in here, they are awestruck. This is why Babar believes in these girls and why he knows they will be champions one day. They have a sense of history and a desire to be part of that history. In contrast, the men's team captain comes in here every day, complaining about some new issue, whether it's a payment he hasn't received, or about the fact that his SUV wasn't allowed into the stadium. Never once has he even glanced at the trophy cupboard. He's more concerned about his latest tweet than about winning trophies.

'Girls, I want to introduce you to an old friend of mine. This is Johnny Cochrane, we used to play Grade cricket together in Australia, and now Johnny is one of the most successful sports agents and marketers in the world. The board has invited Johnny to Lahore to see how we can enhance the profile of the women's team.'

Johnny Cochrane looks like a stereotyped caricature of an Australian Ad man. Big hair, a big smile that shows his perfectly aligned, shiny white teeth, contrasting with his orange perma-tan skin. A pair of blue reflective Oakley sunglasses rests on his head, and his pin striped suit, purple socks, orange tie and bright red suspenders look garishly out of place in the heat of Lahore.

'G'day girls. Congratulations on a fabulous Asia Cup win. Everyone in Australia is talking about it.'

'Really sir? But Australia weren't even in the tournament.'

'That's the point. You're Sanam right? Well Sanam, it was a big deal because you girls became a front-page story in Australia. The media caught on to your tale and not just the sports journos. The underfunded, unfancied Pakistan women's team, forced to sleep in the Feroze Shah Kotla dressing room because the tournament organisers were afraid that they would get lynched by right wing Hindu fanatics, goes out and wins the whole goddamn tournament. Talk about poetic justice. People were won over by the dignified way you conducted yourself and your team. They see a group of courageous young women, led by an articulate and very attractive captain, fight their way through adversity, to win. It helped of course that you had toured Australia earlier this year and cricket fans recognized some of the talented players in the squad, like the two of you. But your story was what made you real box office. For Chrissakes, my 14-year-old niece, when she found out I was travelling to Pakistan, begged me to get your autograph so she could show it off in school. I didn't even realize that she knew where Pakistan was, but she knew. Because of you. Half the bloody schoolgirls in Australia want to be you now.'

'I still don't understand sir. We just played cricket. I'm thrilled that my team has fostered so much goodwill, but why would our Asia Cup win inspire schoolgirls in Australia?'

Johnny Cochrane smiles and looks at Babar. 'Look girls, I've been in this business a long time, and what I can tell you about marketing is that it narrates a story. A story people want to hear. That's our job, we fashion those narratives. And in sport, the most successful stories, the most lucrative stories, are the ones with a compelling narrative. Manchester United being rebuilt by Matt Busby after the Munich air crash, so that 10 years after that fateful day, they won the European cup. Mohammed Ali returning to the ring after years in the wilderness for his principled opposition to the Vietnam war, putting on the fight of the century with Joe Frazier. Lance Armstrong, cancer survivor, winning the Tour De France. Excuse my language, but these kinds of stories are the stuff of marketing men's wet dreams. And your story is in the same category. The beauty about you girls is that you have a fantastic collective story, as well as fascinating individual stories. Sanam, the cool-headed captain, deadly fast bowler, big hitting batswoman, with the looks of a fashion model. Fatima, the coach's daughter who taught herself the perfect batting technique. That spinner you have, what's her name? Sassui? Picked out of obscurity from a village in the desert, never played with a cricket ball till she showed up at national team trials, but spins the ball more than Shane Bloody Warne. This kind of stuff is gold dust in my business.'

Fatima and Sanam look at the strange, orange-faced Australian as if he has just landed from another planet, and look inquiringly at Babar.

'Girls, your success in the Asia Cup took everyone by surprise. Even we weren't aware of the true impact of your victory internationally, until Johnny called me up. We want to raise your profile, both in the domestic market as well as internationally. We really think this will be good for Pakistan cricket and for the country more broadly, especially with the World Cup coming up next month in England. You represent a positive and wholesome image, while your male counterparts, well you know…'

'Ah screw their male counterparts Babs. Nobody wants to know about that bunch of dim-witted losers. Babar asked me to get them some sponsorships on their last tour of Australia. I asked around, but nobody was interested in throwing money at them. Look, let's be brutally honest. Since that World Cup 20 years ago, when your boys got to the final and then choked it or threw it, depending on whose version you accept, your team has been in total decline. Granted, they've still had great players like Babar and FQ, but the issue isn't one of talent. It's reputational. Somehow, the stink of the match-fixing allegations never quite goes away from the men's team. If sponsors are worried that your team is going to throw in the towel for money, they don't want to know. Sports fans are a crazy bunch. They will accept you back even if you are a wife beater or a goddamn rapist, but if they get a sniff that the performances they saw on their TV screens weren't a genuine contest, forget about it. You're dead to them. They just don't want to hear about match fixers.'

Now its Babar's turn to look dumbfounded. 'Hang on a minute Johnny. I thought you said sponsors weren't interested in the men's team because they weren't very good. You never told me back then it was because of match-fixing.'

'Myte, it's got nothing to do with their talent. Last year, I got the Zimbabwean team endorsements, and they got thrashed in every single game they played. I didn't want to tell you because, well, many people cite you as an example of match-fixing. I mean, people haven't forgotten that test match in which you dropped what was it, like 15 catches? And Australia's last pair were able to chase down over a hundred runs for the most improbable win ever?'

There's a pained, and panicked expression on Babar's face, as he nervously looks at Sanam before answering. 'I wasn't a hundred percent fit that day Johnny. How many times do I have to repeat myself over that story? I even went to court to answer those allegations.'

'Babs, Myte, I'm not judging you. But yours wasn't the only case. There was that Sharjah final against India when FQ declared himself fit, but then pulled out half an hour before the match, with no explanation. And then of course there's the big one, the World Cup loss. Those are just the ones I remember off the top of my head. That inquiry tribunal cited dozens of other examples. The match-fixing allegations are a reality that your generation has to deal with. Whether you took a bung or were under the weather that day in Sydney, or whether FQ was 100% fit or just pretending to be injured in that World Cup final, nobody cares about what the reality is. It's perception that matters. And in the perception of fans around the world, and, more importantly, big-name sponsors, your men's teams haven't been kosher for the past 20 years. So nobody's willing to buy that old crap. The girls on the other hand, are a totally different story. Do you know how many requests I've gotten for endorsements for these girls? More than 30. And this is without me even trying to market them. Companies are calling me up and enquiring, just because they know you and I are mates.'

'Excuse me sir, 30 requests from cricket equipment companies?'

'No Fatima, from all sorts of companies. Everything from bras to biscuits. The possibilities are endless with you girls. I don't mind telling you, that with your face Sanam, and your chest, Fatima, I could really put together something special…'

'Johnny!! What the hell!'

'Sorry Babs. My apologies, girls. I didn't mean to sound lewd. But the fact is, your looks have a lot to do with why you're so much in demand. You have a dramatic backstory, you're smart, well spoken, athletic, and extremely attractive. That's just part of the business. You think Maria Sharapova makes $20 million a year just because she wins a lot of tennis matches? Hell no. Look, I'm not saying you girls should pose in thongs or anything like that. Of course I understand the cultural sensitivities around these matters. All I'm saying is, you have to keep an open mind about the marketing potential that you girls have. Especially the two of you. You've got a World Cup around the corner. You're going to be going in as one of the favourites. If you do the right deals, in addition to all the deals I can fix up with the board, I can guarantee that I can get the two of you around 300K each by the end of the tournament. And that's US dollars, not Australian.'

Fatima exhales loudly. She has never even heard of such sums. She isn't even quite sure how much money that would be, after converting it into rupees. Certainly enough to fulfil a lot of dreams.

'Johnny, if you think Fatima and Sanam can individually net those kinds of numbers, then you have to do something for them. There's a lot of local interest as well in the team, but I'm just concerned that the board, and the girls, should not be short-changed in any way.'

'Don't you worry Babs, you leave it to me myte. I'm going to make these girls, and myself of course, very rich in a very short time. Girls, you just concentrate on winning that World Cup. You succeed in doing that, and you can treble the numbers I just gave you. That's the real honeypot. And stay away from those bums in the men's team. Babar, I've got a flight to catch, but we'll stay in touch.'

The tall, technicolour Australian lumbers out of the office, but Fatima and Sanam are silent, as if in a trance. Babar gives them a couple of minutes to allow what Johnny has said to sink in. 'What's wrong girls? Why are you so quiet?'

'Sir, we never realized that any of this could happen. You know none of us got involved in cricket for the money. We all knew there was no money in women's cricket. We never even imagined the kinds of sums this Mr. Johnny was quoting.'

'Yes, I'm sorry about Johnny. He's very...Australian...in his outlook. But he is right. You are sitting on a goldmine. This is your chance. Win this World Cup, and change your lives, and the lives of your families forever. Don't let go of that opportunity. I know, because I've been there. All of us in that World Cup squad were so close to it we could taste it. You know, we were brilliant that entire tournament. Didn't matter who we were playing, or what the match situation was. We just kept winning. Skipper kept telling us that if we believed in ourselves, nothing could stop us from attaining our destiny. And then everything got screwed up in that damn final...'

Babar's eyes glaze over, and the greatest wicketkeeper of his generation turns and looks outside the window onto the green turf of the Gaddafi stadium, his mind a million miles away, distracted by long-subdued memories that have forcibly surfaced.

'Sir? Sir are you alright?'

'Hm? Oh yes, sorry. Just thinking. Anyway, like Johnny said, there's a great future out there waiting for you. And on our part, the board will do everything to ensure that you girls have the best possible preparation for the World Cup. We have agreed to your request, Sanam, to fly the team out to England two weeks before the start of the tournament, to help the girls get acclimatized with the conditions. We will run a conditioning camp before that, here in Lahore, starting next week. On my personal request, the great Faisal Qureshi will join the camp to give all of you some coaching tips and advice on how to deal with pressure situations. The board was also trying to get Tariq Zaman *sahib* to come by and have a talk with you girls as well, but as you know, he unfortunately passed away yesterday.' Sanam is surprised to see Babar's eyes moistening. He coughs, holding back the emotion, before continuing. 'It's funny you know. Calling him Tariq Zaman *sahib* sounds strange. All my life, I knew him only as Skipper.'

Babar pauses and again looks wistfully out the window. The pause is so long that finally it is Sanam who prompts him to go on.

'Uh, sir? You were saying there was something else as well?'

'Oh yes. We have also decided to give all of you a raise in your contracts, as a bonus for the Asia Cup win, and also to bring your contracts closer in alignment to some of the other international teams. All of your travel and accommodation from now on will also be upgraded. No more traveling in economy. Like the men, you will be in First class. Nothing is too good for our girls.'

Sanam can hardly believe her ears. These are all things that she has been fighting for with the board for years, demanding treatment at par with the men's team. And now, in an instant, all her demands have been granted, without any argument. 'Thank you, sir. But how come the board had a change of heart on all these issues?'

Babar looks at her and smiles. 'It's all different now Sanam. You girls have given all of us hope once again. Hope for winning a World Cup. It would be silly of the board to continue to be rigid on these issues. That would have undermined your preparations to win the World Cup. And the board wants nothing to come in the way of that. And when you're in England, if there's anything you need, just call me. In fact, I'll put you in touch with an old friend of mine who lives in London. His name is Saleem Memon. We…uh…used to call him Saleem Euro, because he used to be in the currency trading business. Just call him; he'll sort out anything you need. He's very resourceful, so even if it's something personal, or not directly cricket related, just let him know. He's a huge fan of yours. He's been following the team for a while now and he'll be thrilled to meet you when you get to London.'

'Sir, isn't Saleem Euro the name of a famous bookie? I heard he had been involved in match-fixing. Don't you think it would look bad if we were meeting him?'

Babar seems a bit taken aback by the bluntness of Fatima's question. 'Uh no, no Fatima, it was nothing like that. It was all a big misunderstanding back then. Saleem had some interests in a betting shop in London, that was all. Betting is a legal activity in England, but just because he was friends with some of us, the press started making these allegations that he was a big-time bookie. It was all rubbish. He was never charged with anything. None of us were charged, but just because we were losing on the field, the government of the day got after us, and there was the inquiry commission and all that. He's a good man, Saleem; do meet him, he will be very helpful, especially on a long tour of England.'

Babar rises to signify the end of the meeting. As Fatima walks out the door, he gestures to Sanam to stop a moment, and hands her an envelope.

'Sanam, there's one more thing I'd like you to do. As a personal favour to me. As you know, both of you will be going to Skipper's house to visit his family tomorrow. Could I ask you to give them this letter? It's from me. Please make sure his family gets it.'

'Sure sir, but I'm not too familiar with his family. I know he got divorced from that French woman he was married to some years ago. But I heard his children don't live here, and hasn't his father also passed away? Who would I give the letter to?'

'His sister, Rumessa *Apa*. The *soyem* will be at her house tomorrow, on Meera Khan road, just off St John's Park in Cantt. That's where he lived for the past few years, after he donated his own house for his hospital. Do give her my regards please.'

'You won't come yourself sir?'

'I...It's complicated. I want to go, but my...our relationship... those of us who were in Skipper's World Cup team...became estranged after that tournament. Skipper never said anything himself, but Rumessa Apa wasn't exactly our biggest fan. She blamed us...for a lot of things. Anyway, I think my going would probably be uncomfortable for everyone who's there. But I just wanted to send my condolences, so I wrote that letter. Please do give it to her.'

'Of course sir.'

CHAPTER 5

They say it never rains in Lahore in May. Even if it does, it's certainly never like this. The rain pelts down on the car with the force of a sledgehammer, the harsh thud of the drops hitting the bonnet and roof making a deafening sound. The driver slows to a crawl due to the total lack of visibility. It seems to Sanam that the only way he can continue driving in this storm is by activating some intuitive mental sonar.

She rolls down her window just an inch to get a sense of where they have reached. She barely catches a glimpse of the brown waters of Lahore's famous *Nehr* almost spilling over onto the road, before her green national team blazer is drenched. So great is the flooding that even the canal's regular urchins, who never miss an opportunity to bathe in the dirty water, have decided to give their usual sport a miss in this storm. Sanam worries about getting late for the *soyem* and asks the driver how much longer it will take, but the man simply shrugs his shoulders, nods toward the unsighted windscreen and gets back to his navigation.

To be late for the final rites of Tariq Zaman would be a tragedy. Pakistan has had many captains, but only one Skipper. He is the man credited with changing the nature of the country's cricket. The fearless leader who forged a team out of a talented rabble, who got rid of the nepotism, lack of professionalism and inconsistent performances that had constantly plagued the cricket team for decades, and who pioneered the aggressive, positive tactics that did away with the previous dour, defensive approach, and came to define the Pakistan team of his era.

Skipper was always a man who believed in record-breaking performances. The country's most successful captain ever, with more wins under his leadership than under anyone else; first cricketer from anywhere in the world to take 300 test wickets while also scoring more than 5000 runs; the man with the greatest number of match-winning innings in tests or one-day matches; the man with the bestselling poster in the history of the Pakistani publishing industry. Chances are if you came of age in Pakistan between 1977, which is when Skipper made his debut, and 1995, when he finally hung up his boots, you too bought that poster. If you were a boy, you probably attempted (unsuccessfully, 9 times out of 10) to copy that strange Afro-like hairstyle that Skipper managed to look cool in, despite it having fallen out of fashion in the '70s. At the very least, you turned your collar up and walked around your bedroom as if you had a stick stuck up your ass. Equally, if you were a female born in this period, you have gazed upon that poster at least once, stared into those blue eyes, and willed the glossy image to come to life and propose to you.

Skipper's life resembled the perfect feel good movie, where everything happens just as it should, the nice guy gets the girl, and good always triumphs over evil. Right up until the last act –that accursed World Cup. The one where Pakistan were overwhelming favourites, and Skipper was expected to lead them on a lap of honour to formalize what had already been recognized as their outstanding performances against all comers in the year leading up to the tournament. Of course, that's not what ended up happening, and from there on, the trajectory of Skipper's life had taken a downward turn. Just as everything he had done before the World Cup had effortlessly succeeded, everything after it failed miserably. Like a boxer who takes that one fatal punch that ends an otherwise brilliant career, Skipper never quite recovered from that defeat.

'Oye, what the fuck was that *bhenchodai* yesterday?' Fatima has been quiet since Sanam picked her up in the vehicle that the board has given to them to go for the condolence.

'What do you mean?'

'Why did Babar sir hold you back after the meeting. Did he push you to meet with that *kanjar* Saleem Euro?'

Sanam's eyes widen, and she nods towards the driver, embarrassed that he would have overheard Fatima's coarse language. Fatima shrugs nonchalantly and chuckles. 'Don't worry, it's not the first time *chacha* has heard these kinds of words. He's not as sheltered as you.' Even the old driver looks up from his navigation and smiles at that one.

Sanam purses her lips as if to respond, but lets the comment pass. 'No, Babar sir didn't push me to meet Saleem Euro. He wanted me to give a letter from him to Tariq Zaman *sahib*'s sister because he said he couldn't come to the *soyem* himself.'

'I bet he can't. Skipper's sister hates him.'

'Why?'

'Are you joking? You don't know? Everyone knows. She holds Babar sir and that whole clique of players – Faisal Qureshi, Azhar Abbas, Ovais Tawheed, and Shoaib Abdullah – responsible for destroying Skipper's life.'

'Why? I thought they were all Skipper's boys. Babar sir always said that it was Skipper who discovered every one of them and brought them into the team. He said Skipper fought with the selectors to get him in the side, when they preferred Babar sir's elder brother as the keeper. So why would Skipper's sister hate them all?'

'That was all before the World Cup final. Everything changed afterward. Skipper was bitter because this group, his 'boys', threw the match. The World Cup victory was supposed to be his great triumph. Remember that hospital he wanted to build in honour of his mother?'

'Yes I do remember. I collected money for the hospital when I was in class 7. But it never got built, right?'

'It never got built, because Skipper had banked on the fact that a successful World Cup would generate the donations needed to fund it. And after these players threw the World Cup final, no one wanted to contribute a single paisa to his hospital. Skipper had to retire immediately afterward in disgrace.'

Sanam is quiet for a moment. In a different way, that same World Cup was a seminal moment in her life as well. For it was while watching the brilliance of Skipper's team during that tournament, that she first fell in love with the game. The names that Fatima mentions were the first cricketing gods that Sanam ever worshipped. Of course, none of what Fatima is saying is new to her. She vaguely remembers the match-fixing controversy from that time. She was just 11, too young to comprehend what had happened. She does remember that a lot of people were angry, her father included. He didn't come out of his room for two days, and when he finally resurfaced, he kept muttering, for days, about how 'they' could have done such a thing. But these things did not matter to Sanam at the time. As a new convert to cricket, she was enamoured with the beauty of the game, and not yet invested emotionally in a Pakistani victory. That early innocence protected her from the soul-crushing disappointment that the rest of the country had felt, of having lost a World Cup final, of having come so close yet remaining so far.

'Do you really think they threw that final Fatima? I know that all those players have been dogged with these rumours for 20 years, but I always figured that was something disgruntled fans alleged every time Pakistan lost an important match. Nothing's ever been proved, right?'

'*Yaar*, to be honest, I don't know. I'd like to think it isn't true because all of them were such great players, and it was such a big occasion. But I've heard the stories so many times from people on the club cricket circuit here, from so many people who would be in a position to know, that there must be some truth to them. I know a lot of current and retired national team players who have fixed matches at club level, just for a little *jaib kharch*. So why wouldn't they do it at the international level, when the money on offer from bookies would be a lot more than what a couple of *juwaari*s would offer for a stupid club match? Besides, apart from that final, people talk about so many other dirty matches in those years, especially after Skipper retired. Even that Australian mentioned the test match where Babar *sahib* dropped all those catches. I saw that match on TV. And I remember thinking, as a fellow wicketkeeper, it was just not possible to drop so many catches, unless you were literally having a stroke on the field.'

'No I don't believe that at all. Babar sir would never do anything like that deliberately. I've known him since I first came into the team, ten years ago. He was my first coach. I've never met a more honourable man. I saw that match too. It was the Sydney pitch. It had extra bounce in it, and he played that match without any practice or acclimatization. It's never easy to immediately transition from our slow, low pitches to the bouncy Australian ones.'

'Really? How many catches did I drop on our Australian tour?'

'Well…none.'

'So I guess I acclimatized ok, from our slow, low pitches, huh? And I've played a lot less cricket than Babar sir. If he's so honourable, why does he want us to meet Saleem Euro in London?'

'Why do you keep going on about this Saleem Euro? Why does he matter so much?'

'*Yaar*, you know, sometimes I wish you would get out of this sheltered princess world of yours and get some awareness of the real world! Babar sir lied. Saleem Euro isn't some small-time businessman in London. He is a major bookie. He was rumoured to be one of the bookies who was in with FQ and Babar sir in their heyday.'

'What does that have to do with us? If he is a bookie, he would have asked Babar sir to introduce him to the men's team. Why us?'

'Because we've become big business. The same reason that Australian gave for the commercial interest in us. We're serious contenders to win the World Cup. One of the players at my father's club told me that the bookies in Lahore will bet more money on our matches during the World Cup, than on the men's. Bookies like to bet on the horse that's likely to go far. If you know that the men's team is going to lose in the first round, there's no excitement in the betting.'

Sanam doesn't respond, but opens her window again. The cool rain feels good on her face. Their driver has managed to successfully navigate his way to Cantt, and Sanam can see the shops surrounding Fortress Stadium, as they slow down at the military checkpoint. They take a right and turn into St John's Park. This is one of the oldest neighbourhoods in Cantt, and it still hasn't lost its old-world charm. Ancient trees planted on either side of the road provide almost a complete canopy over their heads. The leaves, looking greener for having been washed, drip ceaselessly with rain water. The houses here are all old-fashioned, mostly bungalows with sprawling lawns. Even the newest ones on the street date back to at least the '70s. There is none of the post-modern construction you see in the city's newer, posher areas, like Defence or Gulberg. The residents of St John's Park have lived here for generations.

There is a line of parked cars in front of one of the oldest houses on the street. A soaked *shamiana*, pitched in the spacious front lawn, sags dangerously in the wind and rain, and cascades water over the low boundary wall, onto the street. The girls step out of their car hoping the soaked tent won't keel over on top of them and, in their haste, step right into a fast-flowing stream snaking its way downhill. They cover their heads with their *dupatta*s, more for protection against the rain than for reasons of modesty. As they enter the front gate, a tall man, walking a couple of paces in front of them, pauses at the front porch of the house, as if unsure where to go. He seems to be looking at an old woman with snow white hair, who is sitting on the floor of the porch, surrounded by a small group of mourners, pouring over copies of the Quran. Sanam assumes that the old woman must be Rumessa Apa, Skipper's sister.

One of the other mourners points out the tall man to the old woman. When she raises her head to look at the man, her eyes betray absolute hate. With a start, she raises herself, in the process dislodging the *dupatta* from her head.

'You! How dare you come here? Have you no shame? You *namak haram*! He gave you everything. Everything! And in return, what did you do? Destroyed his life! Get out! And tell the others that they better dare not come to my house again!'

The tall man stands shell-shocked and motionless for a moment. Then, very slowly and deliberately, he turns around and starts walking toward the gate without a word. In the process, he nearly rams into Fatima and Sanam, and it is then that Sanam recognizes him. He looks older than when she last saw him on TV. There are grey streaks in his signature shoulder-length mane, and the familiar pockmarked face has a wizened look to it. A pair of stylish Ray-Bans hide his eyes, but otherwise, it is unmistakeably Faisal Qureshi, legendary fast bowler, former test captain, one-time protégé of Skipper, and the man who has been Sanam's inspiration for playing cricket.

As he walks past them without acknowledging them, Rumessa Apa's wild eyes turn to their green blazers with the cricket board logo emblazoned on them. 'And what are you bloody board officials doing here? You can just get out as well! You didn't do anything for him when he was alive, now what have you come here for?'

Sanam and Fatima are stunned and look at each other, silently debating whether they should clarify who they are, but both think better of it and turn around and start walking toward the gate. As they stand in the pouring rain, hoping to find where Chacha has parked, a woman from the house comes running after them and taps Sanam on her shoulder.

'Wait, you're Sanam Khan right? I' m so sorry, my aunt didn't recognize you, she thought you were some Board flunkies who had come with Faisal Qureshi. Please, come inside, she is asking you to come back.'

Rumessa Apa is no longer on the porch, and the few remaining mourners also disperse as the intensity of the storm increases. Despite it being late afternoon, the clouds are so dark that the lights have been turned on. Rumessa Apa's niece leads them to a sitting room where the furniture looks as if it hasn't been changed in 50 years. The carpet on the floor is old and musty, and the upholstery on the sofas has become threadbare. Along the walls and shelves, gathering dust, are random bits of cricketing memorabilia. An old stump, a souvenir from some famous test victory, lies on one shelf. A signed, black-and-white picture of Skipper and the West Indian great Gary Sobers is on another shelf. A larger, framed photo of Skipper, dressed formally in a *sherwani*, receiving an award from the dictator General Zia ul Haq, hangs from the wall.

The room is large, with high ceilings, built in the colonial style, to allow for coolness in the long summers. But the storm outside has made the room draughty, and Sanam and Fatima, already drenched from standing in the rain, shiver as they walk in. An ancient gas heater sits where a fireplace used to be, a couple of its bars having been lit to stave off the chill. On one side of the heater sits Rumessa Apa in an ornately carved wooden chair, looking every inch like a Shakespearean crone with a grim expression on her face and her long, snow white hair, no longer restrained by a *dupatta*, descending well below her shoulders and cascading in all directions. She points to the second chair of the pair, on the other side of the heater, and gestures for Sanam to sit there, while her niece seats Fatima on one of the old sofas.

'I apologise for shouting at you earlier girls. I didn't recognize you, I thought you had walked in with that scoundrel. My God, you two are soaked! Mohammed Hussain, bring towels for the girls, they'll catch a chill otherwise. And bring some hot tea.'

A servant hands towels to Sanam and Fatima and they gratefully wipe their hair. 'It's fine Ma'am. No need to apologise. How could you have known who we were? We're sorry for your loss.'

For the first time, a hint of a smile creeps across Rumessa Apa's face as she looks at Sanam intently. 'You know, that used to be Tariq's chair, that one. He would sit there every day, for hours. He'd come in after his morning walk and have his tea and read the newspaper while sitting there. He always still read the sports pages, and the cricket news. God knows why, after all the pain that sport caused him. I wouldn't do it, in fact I haven't followed cricket for 20 years, because I couldn't bear to read about those rascals. Oh, he would lie and pretend he had no interest, and didn't know what was going on with the team. He wouldn't watch any of the matches on TV. But I knew. He would still read all the stories, all the match reports, no matter how badly the team had played. Then, a few months ago, he started telling me about you girls. He had read about your exploits in Australia and he was so excited. I hadn't heard him talk like that about cricket in years. He was so proud of you. He said your captaincy reminded him of himself. And you, Fatima, he said he wished he had a batsman like you playing in that World Cup. You know, in his last days, he was very weak, barely able to hold down his food. The only thing he asked for was a TV, on the day of your Asia Cup final against India. He was so happy that Pakistan won. He was on a ventilator, but I could still see the smile on his face under the oxygen mask. I should be thanking you girls, you gave him back his first love.'

Both girls' hearts swell with pride. After all the struggles, it is the ultimate acknowledgement to hear that the great Skipper rated them so highly.

The servant returns with a tray laden with cups of steaming Kashmiri *chai*, laced with thick blobs of *malai*, and *khatai*s. Rumessa Apa serves both girls herself, her cronishness slowly turning into the kindliness of a favourite aunt. Fatima, being a true Lahori, loves dunking the almond-filled biscuits in her tea, and is about to do so, but restrains herself when she remembers her surroundings. It would be unbecoming of the Pakistan ladies' team vice-captain to be dunking *khatai*s in Kashmiri *chai* while condoling the death of the country's most famous captain. Instead, she stares at the wall opposite her, idly glancing at the memorabilia. One of the items on the shelf is a cricket ball, encased in a glass case, with the words 'Sharjah '92' scribbled on a piece of plaster stuck on the case. Fatima's eyes widen in awe as she realizes where the ball is from. Rumessa Apa watches her and smiles.

'Go on. You can pick it up if you like.'

'Ma'am is that…really…the same ball?'

'Yes, the one he hit for the last ball six.'

'Oh My God. Sanam, it's the ball from the India match. *The* India match. Ma'am, I was 10 years old back then, but I still remember it like it was yesterday. After I made my debut, I bought a DVD recording of the match. I've watched it so many times, I've memorized every ball.' Fatima starts mimicking the commentary. 'Rajan to Zaman. Rajan comes in, pitches it short, Zaman hooks and that's a six!!! Pakistan win! Skipper has sunk India again!' In her excitement, Fatima almost spills her tea.

'Tariq was always so careless about his cricket trophies, but that one his ex-wife forced him to put in a case. Even she realized that one was special. Now I wish I had saved more of them.'

'What happened to them ma'am?'

'That silly French trollop took most of the expensive mementos in the divorce settlement. Tariq had a bunch of them, you know, things like gold goblets and silver cups and what not, in his old London flat. Bloody gold digger! She didn't know what cricket was before she met my brother, but she certainly had an eye for the finest trophies. The other things, you know, like stumps and balls and old pieces of kit from his matches, lay around for years in his house. After the World Cup', Rumessa Apa pauses, trying to compose herself, 'when he, uh, figured out that he wouldn't be able to raise the money for Amma's hospital, he sold most of the things to raise whatever funds he could for the hospital construction. But that was never going to be enough. That's when he decided to move in here. He vacated his own house so it could be converted into a hospital. It obviously wasn't going to be on the scale he had initially envisioned, but he was very clear about the fact that he had given his word to build a hospital, and so many hundreds of people had contributed money for it, that he had to see it through, even if it meant that he would leave no legacy for his own children.'

'Ma'am, where are they? His children?'

'They live in Paris. Their mother remarried soon after the divorce, while she was still young and attractive. Some rich chateau owner, I think. She never enjoyed living in Pakistan, and the pressure and the abuse that came after the World Cup became a convenient excuse for her to leave Tariq. The children were so young when they left, they barely remember their father. They're totally French now. I don't think they even speak English anymore, let alone Urdu or Punjabi. I sent them a message when Tariq died, but I got a text from that witch, saying the children were incommunicado because they were hiking in the Swiss mountains. I didn't see the point of waiting to see if they might come, so we went ahead and buried him. Bloody Frenchies, couldn't even come to give a shoulder to my poor brother's coffin.'

'Ma'am what about the hospital? Is it still running? I haven't heard anything about it in recent years. Maybe we can help raise funds by arranging some charity matches? I am sure Babar sir will get the Board to approve them.'

'Heh. Of course he will. Your Babar 'sir'. He'll do anything to get back in my good books. But I don't want his, or the Board's help. The Board wouldn't return Tariq's phone calls once he retired. Didn't want to go near him because of the stigma of the World Cup. But the actual rascals who did the fixing, your Babar sir and FQ and Ajju and Shoaib, they kept them on in the team. Even made FQ the captain. At the time Tariq wanted their help, he wanted the team to play some charity matches to raise funds, but the board, and the players, were 'concerned' that it would bring back negative memories of the World Cup for the public. It hurt him that his boys were so willing to blame the entire fiasco on him. As if he was the fixer, and not them. He never said anything, but it hurt him. Then the government started giving him trouble. Auditing the accounts of the hospital charity. Sending Tariq income tax notices. Withholding permission for a new gas connection for the hospital. Little, little things. With so many problems, the hospital could never get going, even on the modest scale that Tariq had hoped for. That's when he finally got angry and decided to go into politics. He said if this was what the government did to someone like him, who was trying to do something good, then God knows how they treated ordinary people. He was going to change things. And the people supported him. Oh how they supported him.'

'Ma'am, I remember my father took me and my sisters to Skipper's rally at the Minar-e-Pakistan, because it was close to our house in Shahdara. It was massive. There were thousands of people. My father has never voted in his life, but he took us all to the rally, because Skipper had been his hero and he wanted Skipper to inspire us like he had inspired him.'

'Yes. He inspired us all. We told him people wouldn't come to support him because they still hadn't gotten over the World Cup defeat, even after so many years. But he said people weren't so stupid. They would remember all the positive things he did, and would come for him. And he was right. They came. But that's what scared the 'powers that be'. That Tariq would become someone they couldn't control. So they staged that whole drama, got Ajju to come out in public and say that Tariq had been the ringleader for the fixing in the final. In 20 years of playing cricket, no one had ever made such an accusation against Tariq. Of course, if you throw enough mud on someone, the public starts believing it, no matter how improbable the claims. That's what the 'powers that be' count on. But it just shattered Tariq. He withdrew from the world after that. Didn't want to meet anyone or do anything.'

Rumessa Apa doesn't sob or wail when she says this. She isn't the wailing type. But the tears flow down her cheeks uncontrollably, and her voice is hard, bitter, filled with cold anger. Sanam holds Rumessa Apa's hand, and Fatima gets up to hug her.

'Ma'am, please let us know if there is anything we can do for you. Treat us like your own daughters.'

The old woman blesses them and kisses their forehead. 'Thank you for coming girls. Thank you for remembering him.'

*

The rain has abated but the dark clouds still remain overhead, during the drive back home. Washed and scrubbed in the storm, Lahore looks cleaner and more vibrant.

'Sanam, promise me one thing.'

'What?'

'Whatever else happens, no matter what Babar sir or anyone else says, we will not meet this *kanjar* Saleem Euro. I don't want these *bhenchod* bookies coming near our team. Look at what they did back then. They ripped apart a world class team and destroyed a good man in the process. Promise me, you won't let this man in.'

Sanam stops staring out of the window at the emerging rainbow, and tries to focus on Fatima, but suddenly, without warning, tears start to flow from her eyes. She feels an immense sadness. She doesn't know why, after all, she has only just met this old woman. And Skipper was hardly a young man cut down in his prime, for the death to be particularly tragic. But the sadness comes from realizing the unfolding of a real tragedy. The story of how petty-minded men brought down an icon.

CHAPTER 6

She can feel his eyes boring into her, looking at every little twitch and movement that her body makes. And it makes her nervous. Sanam usually loves practice sessions. She loves being in the nets, in heat or cold, hour after hour, testing her body, honing her skills. She has never gotten nervous in front of coaches or selectors standing there, watching and assessing her. It has always given her an adrenaline rush, knowing that she had to perform on demand.

But this is different. This is not just any old coach or selector watching her. This is Faisal Qureshi, the great FQ, the man who is the reason for her playing cricket. FQ has been her god ever since she started watching cricket. The first match Sanam ever watched was a group game from *that* World Cup. It was a Friday afternoon, and her father was home, watching the game. She had been nagging him to take her out, but he handed her a bottle of Coca Cola, and promised her he would take her for a drive if she sat quietly and watched the match with him for an hour. By the end of the hour, there was no need to go out anymore. Sanam was enthralled.

The game itself wasn't a particularly good contest. Pakistan played Sri Lanka at Derby, but this was a Sri Lankan team without the machismo and confidence that would allow them to win the next World Cup. So it was a pretty one-sided contest, with Skipper's team ultimately winning quite easily. But what captured Sanam's imagination was Faisal Qureshi's bowling. He couldn't have been older than 22, thin and lanky, his shoulder-length mullet not yet having morphed into the more suave hairstyle of his later years. But he could make the ball do things others could only imagine.

His bowling action was a mini concert, starting with a jog slowly building into a sprint, the crescendo increasing with his leap at the crease, and then the final explosion as the ball was released with the pace and accuracy of a heat-seeking missile, to wreak havoc on an unsuspecting batsman. To this day, Sanam remembers one over from that match, when FQ bowled six completely different balls to the batsman Kalpage. Each one was unplayable in a totally different way. Kalpage, one of the finest batsmen ever to play for Sri Lanka, seemed bewitched, as if FQ had cast some voodoo spell on him that made him forget his technique and grope for the ball like a blind man. Though Kalpage survived, he was so unnerved that he lobbed a simple catch to mid-off in the next over.

FQ had everything: the skill to control the ball, to swing it either way, new or old, and the pace to deliver a swinging ball with unerring accuracy at 90 miles per hour. In that same Sri Lanka game, FQ took three wickets, each one bowled, in exactly the same way, the batsman missing an inswinging yorker. If you saw the replays of those wickets with the mute button on, you would have thought they were replays of the same dismissal, such was their uniformity. Over the years, there were hundreds more victims, as the enduring image of FQ for fans was *that* ball, spread-eagling a batsman's stumps.

For Sanam, an FQ spell was an operatic performance, filled with beauty and the promise of witnessing something truly special. Once, in college, she dumped a boyfriend, on the spot, for suggesting that continuing to make out with him was a preferable exercise than walking out of the dorm in the middle of a freezing night, to go to a Common Room in another building, just to see FQ bowl.

In this context then, her nervousness is justified. Especially as she continues to mask her injury, the side-strain she has been carrying for the past few months. With the World Cup coming up in England, she doesn't want to give the selectors the slightest excuse to even consider benching her. For the most part, she bowls steadily, well within herself, slowly building up her strength. It is only the last few balls of the session that she ups the ante, hurling down a couple of express bouncers that startle the batter, the elegant leftie Ayesha Mufti. Sanam has done this often, bowling injured in the nets. It's an occupational hazard for a tearaway fast bowler. You tend to get injured so frequently, you have to ration your performances to lengthen your career. She knows she is good enough to fool the coaches, even Babar sir, who shouts his encouragement and his general satisfaction about her form from the sidelines.

FQ lingers, even after the other dignitaries walk back to the air-conditioned comfort of their offices. As she packs up her kit, he approaches her. It crosses Sanam's mind that growing older has made FQ even better looking, if that were possible. The lankiness of his youth has gone, along with the mullet, replaced by a more muscular frame, and greying locks that still flow down to his shoulders. Accompanied by the hipster, tight, fitted T-shirt and jeans, and the collection of bands on his wrist, he looks like an ageing, yet eternally cool rockstar, a healthier Keith Richards perhaps, without the years of drug and alcohol abuse.

'Sanam. Hi, I'm Faisal Qureshi.' He walks and talks with a confidence that can only come from having been one of the most talented players of all time. He proffers his hand to her, unusual on its own, since most men tend not to do that with a woman in Pakistan.

'Of course sir, I know who you are.'

'Please, none of this 'sir' bullshit. My friends call me FQ. And I'm a huge fan of yours. You've done a magnificent job with the girls. Also, well bowled in the nets.'

'Thank you, sir…I mean FQ.'

'I noticed that your bowling action was more open-faced today than when I've seen you on TV. Are you injured?'

'No sir, not at all.'

FQ smiles and winks at her. 'Listen, I've had enough side strains in my career to be able to spot one from ten miles away. Even if Babar and your coaches can't see it. Piece of advice, if you do want to hide it during practice, be more sideways, but bring your arm in from a lower angle to put less pressure on the injured side. And take two Neurofens before the nets. Trust me, no one will be able to spot the difference.'

'But…you spotted it.'

'I spotted it because I have been doing the same thing for the past 30 years. I know what it's like to play when you're less than fully fit. For fast bowlers like us, it's rare to ever be 100%. There are always some niggles. If we were to pull out of matches for every minor injury like the batsmen do, we would never get on the field in the first place. And don't worry, your secret is safe with me. I'll give you the number of a very good physio in London. He used to be the team masseur when I played county cricket for Middlesex. He does these heat treatments that'll sort out your side in no time.'

'Thank you, sir.'

'I told you, it's FQ. But jokes apart, we're all very proud of what you've achieved with this team. You've given some hope back to the fans in this country.'

'Thank you. Your speech to us earlier today was truly inspirational. I know a lot of the girls really appreciated it.'

'Hey, that's one thing we retired cricketers are good for, talking. In fact I wanted to have a chat with you, about your experience as a captain and as a fast bowler. Are you still around in Lahore for a few days or are you flying back to Karachi?'

'I'm here till the team leaves for England.'

'Great. Why don't we have dinner tomorrow night. You're staying at the Avari, right? You like Japanese? We can go to Fuji. See you there at 7:30.'

'Uh...sure.'

*

Fifteen minutes before the appointed time for her dinner date, Sanam is in a state of panic. The reason for her panic is of course, trying to figure out whether indeed, it is a dinner 'date', or just dinner. It's unheard of for one of the male cricketers to ask their female counterparts out for dinner. Admittedly, FQ is far removed from the troglodytes currently populating the men's team, but still, his somewhat brazen request has taken Sanam by surprise.

And it's not that she finds anything distasteful in going for dinner with FQ. Truth be told, that has been a fantasy of hers since the age of about 15. Faisal Qureshi's decision to get rid of his mullet in the mid-1990s coincided with the onset of Sanam Khan's puberty, and he suddenly went from being just her favourite cricketer, to her heartthrob. Sanam still remembers the tinge of jealousy she would feel back in those days every time she read the tabloids and saw reports of some dalliance of his with a Bollywood actress or a blonde Australian beach surfer.

So there is a nervous excitement as she dresses for dinner. But this brings her back to her original conundrum, over whether this is a professional dinner, or the realization of a dormant teenage fantasy. Unsure of what impression to give him, she has spent the last hour applying makeup, then removing it, then reapplying it. She debates between the extremes of dressing in her Pakistan team tracksuit, or an extremely fashionable sleeveless *kurta shalwar*. Ultimately, after unpacking everything in her suitcase, she decides on a T-shirt and a pair of tight fitting designer jeans. Casual enough. But then she adds the final touch. A pair of killer heels that she knows would make any man's head turn. Perfect.

She hurries down to the restaurant, conscious that she is five minutes late, something that is a cardinal sin for her. She finds him already there, sitting in a corner table overlooking the swimming pool. Everything about him seems effortless, from the way he looks – which Sanam has to admit is still stunning after all these years – to the way he conducts himself, graciously signing an autograph for a waiter whose idolization of FQ overcomes his fear of incurring the displeasure of his restaurant manager.

He sees her and waves her over, greeting her with unexpected familiarity by nonchalantly kissing both her cheeks in a very European way. She likes his frankness, but also blushes and quickly casts a guilty glance around the room to see if anyone has noticed their interaction.

'Hi Sanam. Wow, you're looking stunning.'

In a heartbeat, his compliment makes all her deliberations over what to wear, worth the effort. She wants to shout out, or at least high-five herself, but she limits her reaction to a nervous smile.

'Thank you si…I mean FQ. I'm…uh…not really used to doing this sort of thing. It's just that, you know, the other male cricketers don't do this.'

'What sort of thing? Have dinner with a colleague?'

'Well, I mean, yes. Or even talk to us. I once met Hasan Kakayzai before the start of a one-dayer in Dubai. I just went up to him to wish him good luck, and he turned around and said he thought women should restrict themselves to the kitchen and not bother about playing cricket.'

'Kakayzai is an arrogant prick. Always has been. I wouldn't mind if he actually backed it up with some skill. But giving a performance once in every ten matches is hardly consistent. I've heard the only reason the board keep him around is because apparently the Taliban love him because he's a Pathan, and they've promised not to attack cricket grounds as long as Kakayzai is captain. Now of course he puts on all these airs, with his Ducati bikes and his designer clothes. But I remember when he broke into the team. We were on tour in India, I was the captain, and he came to me and asked me how to use the commode in the bathroom. He was that clueless. Don't worry about people like him. Shall we order? I know the chef, he does a great special salad for me, and his Teppanyaki is out of this world.'

His smile is infectious, and she remembers it has always been one of the things that she has liked most about him. He also has a knack for putting people at ease. In a matter of minutes, she has forgotten her nervousness as he engages her, talking to her about cricket, about fast bowling, about being a captain. It is the sort of discussion she has always wanted to have with a senior player, but was never able to because every other male cricketer except Babar sir deemed it beneath their dignity to talk to her. What makes it even more special is that she is finally having this chat with the one player she wanted to engage with above all others.

She finds herself hanging on his every word, laughing at his jokes, all the while staring into his eyes. His demeanour encourages her to drop her guard, something she seldom does with strangers. But somehow, he doesn't seem like a stranger. He's like someone she has known all her life.

Their conversation is interrupted by two school girls who approach their table expectantly, mobile phone in hand. Sanam assumes they have come to get a picture with FQ, so she offers to take the picture and points the girls to his side of the table. But they remain standing in their place, facing her.

'I think it's your photo they want Sanam. They're a bit young to remember me. Isn't it girls? You want a selfie with Sanam ma'am?'

The girls nod vigorously in unison and FQ takes the mobile phone to snap the picture. As the girls depart, Sanam notices that the surrounding tables have been observing them, and a spontaneous round of applause breaks out for her.

FQ smiles at her and picks up his glass of juice to toast her. 'So? How does it feel to be the new superstar of Pakistan cricket?'

'I...uh...I'm not sure. It's a bit overwhelming. And a bit unnerving, to know that people are looking at you all the time. How do you get used to something like that?'

He laughs again. 'When I started playing, it was a bit easier because everyone didn't have mobile phone cameras. But it started getting bad towards the end of my career. One thing you learn to do is never to step outside unless you're perfectly made up or attired. My wife once made the mistake of going down to the breakfast room in our hotel in Sharjah in her pyjamas and without her makeup on. It was her bad luck that a photographer took a snap, and the picture was carried the next day in every newspaper and magazine in the country. She was so embarrassed, and they never let her live that down. They called her ugly duckling, and God knows what else. I felt really bad for her, because at the time, we were already living under a microscope, and the press making fun of her certainly didn't help. But don't worry, a pretty girl like you won't have this problem.'

'Was that…around the time of…you know…'

'The match-fixing inquiry? Yes.'

'I'm sorry, I didn't mean to pry.'

'Not at all. I'm used to it. It's one of the questions I'm asked most frequently. It was just an unfortunate episode, and very difficult for those of us who were stuck in the middle of it. I suppose it may have been relatively easier for me, because by the time the inquiry began, I was already planning on retiring. I'd been having problems with my back for a few years, so I was winding down anyway. It just left an unpleasant taste, to feel that the press and board were trying to hound me out. I think it was tougher for some of the younger guys, who had just come into the team.'

'What did it feel like, constantly being accused of this kind of stuff? I don't know how I could take it if aspersions were cast on me every time the team lost a match.'

'I suppose you get used to it. Sort of. You've got to remember, we are a very immature sporting nation. We always need an external factor to blame when we lose. By the time the inquiry commission rolled around, it was the third World Cup in a row that I had played in, in which fixing allegations came out the moment we lost a match. Each time the fans wanted to have someone to take their frustration out on. The first time round, the focus of their anger was Skipper, so I escaped lightly. A big crowd stoned his house, while I was able to get away with someone painting graffiti on my gate. But the next two times, because I was the captain and the main player, I bore the brunt of it. And what made it worse that third time was that we lost to India. An unforgiveable sin, in the eyes of our fans. That World Cup cost me two cars and a wife. Still can't figure out which of those was the greater loss. Heh.'

'You can be so dismissive about your wife leaving you?'

'I wasn't, for a long time. It hurt me a lot, because I fell in love with her when I was just a teenager. She was a student in NCA. Her class used to go to the Bagh-e-Jinnah ground to sketch stuff, and I saw her there because I used to practice there. This was when I first broke into the team. She was something else. Very bold, almost haughty. And boy was she hot! She was the prettiest girl I had ever seen! I was intimidated about just talking to her for the longest time. My English wasn't very good, and she had gone to the best schools in Lahore. But we fell in love. For the longest time, her family didn't think I was good enough to marry her. I was just starting out, there was no guarantee I would become a star. But we were both determined to be together, and so we got married. Which is why her attitude when the troubles began was so hurtful. We had been through tough times together, but it seemed that she didn't want to fight for us anymore. If someone isn't willing to stand by you in your time of trouble, what's the point of being in love with them? She didn't want to stay because of the pressure of the match-fixing allegations. She couldn't take the constant abuse anymore. I tried my best to salvage my marriage; in fact that was also one of the reasons why I decided to retire. I thought being out of the public eye would allow us to rebuild our relationship. But she said the rumours would never go away and she wanted to be free of the baggage.'

'I'm sorry. It sounds really unfair. I always thought that. During those World Cups, I would fight with anyone who said you guys were…throwing matches. It used to really make me angry, because people pass these comments without having any understanding of what a player has to go through, mentally and physically, when you're representing your country.'

'Thank you for that. And thank you for defending my honour for so many years! What happened, happened. I'm not the sort of person who spends time regretting stuff. The allegations affected all our lives. After the inquiry report blamed him, Ajju became really weird, not trusting anybody, not wanting to meet anybody from the cricket world. Shoaib became a Moulvi. And Babar spent all his time trying to justify every bad decision he took, to convince people that it wasn't deliberate. How pointless. In that respect I'm proud of the fact that I didn't go through any radical transformation. I am pretty much still the guy I used to be. A little beat up, but my core values are the same. I only wish I had gotten the opportunity of playing one World Cup without being worried that one dropped catch would kickstart the match-fixing rumours again.'

'I'm also sorry for what happened that day at Skipper's house. Fatima and I…you probably didn't see us, but we were walking in as you walked out. That was harsh.'

'I did see you guys that day. It's just that it was a bit embarrassing, being kicked out like that by Rumessa Apa. I loved Skipper. We all loved him. I'm sorry he felt the way he did, towards the end. But I can put my hand on my heart and say that I never gave anything less than 100% in any match I played for him.'

'Was he angry at you? After that final?'

'He…he just couldn't fathom what happened to us that day. None of us could. You know, we had played so well for so long, we believed we were champions in waiting. That day at Lord's, when everything started going against us, we just couldn't compute how this could be happening to us, and the Australians walked all over us. We didn't show the requisite humility, and in cricket, if you don't do that, the game humbles you. Anyway, I think it was such a shock for Skipper, that after a while, he started believing the rumours that people were spreading about a bunch of us having thrown the match. He didn't have evidence, so he never confronted us, but he just became distant. And then Ajju pulled that silly stunt at the behest of the intelligence agencies, making those false claims that Skipper had been the one involved in match-fixing. Ajju was lying and the Agencies only made him do it because they wanted to sabotage Skipper's political career, but Skipper thought all of us were behind it, just because Ajju was still friendly with us, even though we had nothing to do with his stupidity.'

'What really happened that day at Lords?'

'It was a perfect storm. We lost the toss, and Australia decided to bat. It had rained heavily the night before, right up till the morning. The run ups were muddy and slippery, and as a result Skipper and I couldn't get any rhythm when we ran into bowl. OT, who had bowled us to victory in the semi-final, pulled out on the morning of the match with an injury. By the time Shoaib came on to bowl his spin, the ball was a bit wet and he couldn't grip it, and I just couldn't get my radar right, so the two of us gave away too many runs in the last few overs. Then, when our guys batted, the tension of the occasion just got to them. We just froze. Skipper tried his best, but it wasn't enough. It could have happened to anyone. It should have happened to the Australians, because they were the more inexperienced team. But it happened to us. That's fate. And since that day, those of us who played that match, had to bear that cross for the rest of our careers.'

Sanam is quiet and for a long moment, stares at the glass of water on the table.

'You don't have to feel uncomfortable Sanam. Go on, ask the question. It's what everyone wants to know. Whether we actually threw the match.'

'Actually, that wasn't what I was thinking at all. I just...the enormity of it all just struck me. I...we're going into a World Cup. I've never had to deal with expectation, because no one ever expected anything of my team. But now, we've won, we've proven ourselves, and all these people, the people in this room, the board, the millions who watch on TV, they think we can win. They want us to win. They won't accept anything less. But what if we can't? I mean, you guys tried your best, but sometimes, as you said, luck isn't with you. My girls and I have never dealt with this kind of pressure before.'

'That's where you earn your salary as a captain Sanam. You have to absorb the pressure. Don't let it get to your girls. Tell them to continue playing with the same freedom of spirit that got them in this position in the first place. Always remember, it's just another game of cricket, like the thousands that you've played over the years. You need the same skills to win at Lord's, as you need to win a gully match. The more you think about where you are, and what will happen if you win or lose, the more confused you'll get. I always maintain that in that World Cup, despite the fact that we played well in the early rounds, the one distraction that we had at the back of our minds was Skipper's hospital project. He had invested so much into it emotionally, he was so focused on it, that the rest of us started feeling nervous because we didn't want to disappoint him. The signs were there in some of the earlier matches as well. Babar won us the game against West Indies off the last ball, Ovais bowled out the Kiwis in another match we should have lost. Skipper didn't pick up on it because he was so involved in the fundraising plans for the hospital that I felt for the first time, he wasn't there mentally for us. I wish he hadn't gotten us all so involved in the project. We didn't need that hovering over our heads at that time. God! That's a horrible thing to say isn't it?'

'No. No it isn't. I know exactly how you feel.'

They have been talking for such a long time, the restaurant has emptied and the waiter who so guiltily asked for FQ's autograph at the start of the evening, stands at a discreet distance from their table, with bill in hand.

'Wow, I didn't realize we had been here so long.'

'Yes, time seems to fly when you're having fun. I suspect that if the head waiter hadn't been a fan, they would have thrown us out a while ago. Still, he got a great story out of it. I'm sure he's going to finish his shift and tell everybody he knows about the 'affair' between Faisal Qureshi and Sanam Khan.'

Sanam blushes a bright red, once again taken aback by FQ's forthrightness.

'How do you deal with something like that? I mean, you're very casual about this kind of stuff.'

'Trust me, when you've been accused of far worse things, as I have, you become casual about the petty stuff. It's not worth fretting over. And at least in this particular case, they'll finally be pairing me with someone pretty. A few years ago, this Urdu tabloid ran a story claiming I had been caught by the police after jumping out of the house of Lahore's leading transvestite at three in the morning. When my mother read that story, she called me and asked me why my standards had fallen so much!'

Sanam laughs loudly at the joke, all the while trying to mask her excitement at FQ's compliment.

'Thank you for this…Faisal. I had a lot of fun.'

'I'm glad. Hopefully we can meet up again in England during the World Cup. I'll be there working as a commentator, here's my number, give me a call when you get there. I'll show you some of the dives we used to hang out in when I played for Middlesex. And good luck with the injury. Talk to my old masseur, like I told you. He'll sort you out. And if there's anything else I can do, let me know.'

Well, you could kiss me for starters, and make a 15-year-old fantasy come true, thinks Sanam. But she doesn't verbalise her wish, and instead walks very chastely with him to the hotel lobby. As he waves her goodbye and walks out to the car park, she can't help herself from turning around and casting a final, guilty glance at his perfect ass.

CHAPTER 7

England is wet and gloomy, as it often is in May. It means that Sanam is unable to get her team as much outdoor practice as she would have wanted. Having played league cricket here for years, she is used to the conditions, but she realizes that the girls will need a lot of practice on typically English pitches to adjust their games. So it doesn't help that their first couple of practice games are washed out.

Still, everything else seems to be working out. The board remains true to its word, and the girls are given every resource they need. For the first time, the support staff around the women's team outnumbers the men's. Instead of being put up in the kind of motels and college dormitories that they have become accustomed to, the team is housed in a five-star hotel, along with all the other teams. Since most of Pakistan's matches in the group stage of the competition are in or around London, the board feels it is better for the girls to have a base to travel back and forth from, instead of packing and unpacking their bags every two days. It lends an air of stability to the team.

As for the girls themselves, they are slowly adjusting to their elevated circumstances. Sanam enjoys watching the awe and wonderment that Ayesha Mufti and Sassui Memon feel when they are seated in the business class cabin for the first time on the flight to London. They are the youngest members of the squad, still in their teens, and Sanam plans for them to be her secret weapons in this World Cup. Apart from herself and Fatima, the two girls are the most talented players in the team. Ayesha is the left-handed batswoman who doesn't seem to get fazed in any kind of situation, and who plays every innings with a devil-may-care attitude, as if a one-day international in Australia has no greater significance than a club game in Lahore. That pretty much seems to be her philosophy on life, and while her laxity in all things is a constant irritant for Fatima, who keeps wanting to discipline her, Sanam knows this is the quality she needs if they are to win this World Cup. It's what FQ spoke about, the ability to not be overwhelmed by the occasion, and that's why Ayesha is central to Sanam's plans.

Sassui is a different story. Hers is the latest fairytale story of Pakistan cricket. The daughter of a farmer in rural Sindh, she taught herself spin bowling just by watching TV highlights of matches. Since there was nobody to play with, she perfected her art bowling an old tennis ball against the back wall of the house. There was no opportunity to play any kind of matches, because there were no women's teams in her native Sajawal. The concept of girls playing cricket was as unique to the local residents as walking on the moon. And she would have gone unnoticed had Nadia Malik, one of the fringe members of the team, not accidentally discovered her while playing a friendly game with her cousins during a family picnic. Sassui's ability to spin the ball was so prodigious that Nadia had to report it to Babar sir. Despite her absolute lack of experience of any first-class cricket, she was summoned to team trials in Karachi, where Sassui, bowling with a proper cricket ball for the first time in her life, had out-bowled everyone else, knocking over Fatima's stumps twice in one session.

But despite her sudden elevation to the national team, and her impressive performances in Australia and India, Sassui remains at heart a wide-eyed farm girl. Sanam realizes that and has nurtured her like a child, shielding her from the media, fans, the board, anything that might spook her. Their relationship has become so close, that Sassui calls her *addi*, sister, in her native Sindhi. These girls are the future of this team, so Sanam protects them like a lioness protects her cubs, until such time as they are able to face the big bad world of Pakistan cricket on their own. That will be her legacy.

The last few weeks have been nerve-wracking. Sanam has sacrificed prioritizing her own fitness to help the girls adjust mentally and technically on this tour. She still hasn't been able to go to FQ's masseur to work on her side strain. She has captained several tours in the past, but has never experienced the frenzy of a World Cup. So many things to organize, so many people wanting to talk to her. She would have gone crazy by now if it wasn't for FQ. She ran into him in the hotel lobby the day they arrived, and since then, they have been speaking to each other on the phone every day. It's the part of her day that Sanam looks forward to most. They talk about cricket, but also other things. He tells her about his ex-wife, and she tells him about her battles with her mother. There is nothing romantic or inappropriate in their conversations, at least not yet, but it is certainly the beginning of something special.

Waiting for the tournament to start just adds to the pressure, and for Sanam, Pakistan's opening game against South Africa at the Oval cannot come soon enough. The team returns to their hotel from their final practice session, curtailed again due to the incessant rain. Sanam isn't sure how much of an impact weather conditions have had on their preparations, but one good sign is the team's morale and humour, which has never been better. As they walk into the hotel lobby, they run into the Indian team going out for their practice. The Indian captain DP greets Sassui warmly, and poses for a selfie with her and Ayesha Mufti. The girls excitedly catch up with Fatima and Sanam in the elevator.

'*Addi*, look, I got a picture with DP! DP is so nice!'

Fatima sniggers. 'If I were you, I wouldn't go around telling people you like DP so much.'

'Why Fatima *baji*?'

'Because in English porno films, DP means double penetration.'

The other girls in the elevator double over laughing, and even Sanam betrays a wry smile, as Fatima explains in graphic detail, the anatomical implications of DP to a shocked Sassui.

Sanam is glad to reach her room, as it means she doesn't have to speak to anyone else till the morning. She smiles in anticipation of a hot shower and her daily evening call with FQ. But just as she takes off her cricket boots, there is a knock on the door. She warily opens the door to find a curious pair of men staring back at her. The older man is short and plump, dressed in a shiny suit, his shirt unbuttoned almost to his waist, a pair of designer sunglasses perched above his hairless eyebrows, and wearing enough gold chains and rings to give Mr.T a run for his money. The other man is younger and with his suit-less waistcoat, peroxided hair, light coloured eyes and stylishly trimmed beard, looks like he's just walked out of a boy band audition.

'Sanam Khan? I'm Saleem Memon. Saleem Euro? Babar bhai told you about me? May we come in?' It's the older man who speaks first.

Before Sanam can answer properly, the two men have already entered her room. The younger man places a large green Harrod's bag on her coffee table. Saleem Euro takes out a huge orange Hermes box from the bag, and hands it to Sanam.

'First of all, I just wanted to give you this little present as a token of my appreciation. Babar *bhai* must have told you, I am a big fan of the women's cricket team. A big fan. And you are my favourite player.'

As Sanam stares at the orange box in her hands, still stunned by Saleem Euro's sudden appearance, he takes the lid off the box, and takes out the most elegant handbag that she has ever seen. Admittedly, she has never been a fashionista like her other two sisters, but even she knows enough to understand that the bag must be extremely expensive. Euro strokes the smooth leather like a James Bond villain, nodding vigorously towards Sanam, encouraging her to partake in the stroking as well.

'Uh, Saleem *sahib*, yes Babar sir did tell me about you, and thank you so much for this, but I can't accept such an expensive gift…'

'Sanam, don't worry about the expense. This is nothing. By Allah's grace, I have a huge import export business. *Huge*. The almighty has given me a lot. I have done so much over the years for the men's teams, buying them watches, designer clothes, even cars. This is negligible in comparison. I really wanted to do something for you. Uh, may I sit?'

'Sorry, of course, please sit.' The two men sit on the one sofa in the room, while Sanam plonks herself on the bed opposite them, still awkwardly holding the orange package and acutely embarrassed that her room is a mess, with team shirts, track bottoms, bras and panties strewn across the floor and the bed.

It's almost as if Saleem Euro has read her mind. 'Sanam, please don't feel uncomfortable. Just think of me as an elder brother. Anything else you need, let me know. Is there anyone else on the team that needs anything? Bags, gift items, mobile phones? Anything at all, just let me know. On every tour of England, the men's team is very particular about halal food, so I arrange to have food delivered to their practice sessions and their matches. Do you girls also need that?'

'Thank you, sir, but no. Most of the girls aren't very strict about halal food, and the ones that are, just eat vegetarian or fish instead. Sir, again I don't think I can accept this…'

'Shh, I won't hear of it. It's my gift, to you. A brother can't give his sister a gift? No, don't insult me by returning it. *Haan*, if you don't like it, I'll give you the receipt, exchange it for something you like better. You want any of your friends to get a bag? Fatima Shah, maybe, hmm?'

Saleem Euro fishes in his pocket for and takes out a crumpled receipt, handing it to Sanam. Curious about the cost of the bag, she can't help taking a look, and gasps audibly when she sees a figure of £5000. Euro ignores her reaction completely and leans toward her conspiratorially, lowering his voice to a whisper.

'I also take care of some of the men's team's 'other' needs. Very discreetly.' Euro tilts his head towards his companion, the boy band reject with the impossibly chiselled cheekbones, who stares into space, as if totally oblivious to the conversation. 'Let me know if you have any such requirement. Don't be shy, everyone has needs, it's no problem.'

Sanam's eyes widen in shock, as the implication of Euro's statement settles in. Before she is even able to articulate a coherent response, Euro continues his quick-fire dialogue. He asks her questions as if he is the chairman of selectors, rather than an overenthusiastic fan.

'*Acha* tell me, how is the team condition? Everybody fit for tomorrow's match?'

'Uh, yes.'

'Good. Very good. And you'll play what? The same team as in the Asia Cup? Fatima, Ayesha Mufti, Nadia bibi, the spinner Sassui? And will you play Farzana as the fifth bowler, or that other girl, Nida?'

'I uh, don't know yet. I'll uh, have to see the pitch.'

'Hmm. Good idea. Good idea. And any indications of what the pitch will be like?'

'I...uh...am not sure.'

'Hmm.' Saleem Euro turns to his companion and signals for him to leave the room. 'Look Sanam, I am sure Babar must have told you, he and I had a very good relationship during his playing days. I always arranged some extra pocket money for him, and he helped out with little titbits, nothing that important, but stuff that is very useful for gamblers, when they are trying to decide what to bet on. You see, in addition to my import export business, I run a small, legal betting operation as well, and I like to give my customers the most complete information before they place their bets. That's why it's always good to know these things, like the state of the pitch, weather conditions, how you think the pitch will play if it rains. You know what I mean? That's why I ask these questions. *Acha* forget this, tell me, what do you plan to do if you win the toss?'

'I haven't decided. We'll assess conditions in the morning and then figure out what to do.'

'Hmm. Good, good, very sensible. *Acha*, if you do win the toss, I think put South Africa in to bat first. Definitely.'

'I, uh, haven't given it any thought yet. Sir...'

'Not sir. *bhai*. Saleem *bhai*. Say it, say it.'

'Saleem *bhai*. I...uh...think you should probably go now, Saleem *bhai*, I've got to rest, it's an early start for us tomorrow.'

'Ya, ya, off corse. You need your beauty sleep before big match. You rest, I'll go now, but if you need to get in touch, here, take this iPhone. It's got my number in it already, use it while you're here in England. I'll call you on this number and you can call me.'

As he reaches for the door, he shoves the mobile phone into Sanam's hands, clasping her wrists for a brief moment.

'Listen, think about the toss. Put South Africa in if you win it. I'm very happy to have the same arrangement with you that I used to have with Babar. You can make some good shopping money in this tournament. $5000 just on this toss. Think about it.'

'Uh...*ji* Saleem *bhai*. I will.'

*

When Sanam awakes the next morning, she feels sore. The encounter with Saleem Euro has kept her awake most of the night. She is unsure of what to do. In her anxiety, she doesn't even speak to FQ. She switches off her own mobile phone, and the one Euro thrust into her hands, so no one will contact her, hoping somehow the problem will go away by itself. But in the morning, it still confronts her, taunting her, staring at her, in the form of the big orange Hermès box. She has thought all night, of what to do. The obvious answer is to inform the authorities, her own team management, and the International Cricket Council's anti-corruption unit. But two things hold her back from doing the obvious. One is Babar sir's connection to Saleem Euro. She would have to report that as well, if she were to report this incident. And that would, surely be, after all the years of rumours and allegations, the end of his career, and his dignity. She owes him too much to become the instrument of his downfall. Second, is the faint aura of menace that Saleem Euro exuded when he spoke to her. As if he expected her to obey his wishes on the toss, or on accepting payments, or else. It's the aura of a man used to getting his way, by hook or by crook. It wouldn't be correct to say it scares Sanam, who is no wallflower by any standard, but it does unnerve her and make her think twice.

Having slept barely two hours, Sanam has no idea what the time is. She is forced out of bed by the shrill ringing of the hotel telephone. It's the team coach, sounding manic and informing her that everyone else is already on the team bus, ready to go to the ground. Sanam jumps up and dresses hurriedly, not even bothering with a shower, before rushing out of her room. The problem of the big orange box will have to wait for now.

As she boards the bus, she is greeted by anxious looks. Everyone in the team knows Sanam is never late for anything. The assumption, which is supported by her seemingly shattered appearance, is that there must be something to worry about if Sanam is in such a state. Suddenly a hush falls over the rest of the team, now worried that their unflappable captain, upon whom all the girls are so dependent, looks so spooked. Fatima is the only one to make a comment as Sanam settles into her seat, near the front of the bus.

'Looks like Sanam has also become a fan of DP since yesterday. Who was the *launda*, captain?'

The joke breaks the tension and the other girls return to their earlier high spiritedness. All except Sanam, whose mind remains elsewhere. Her shock at last night's events is slowly turning into anger. How dare Saleem Euro be so presumptuous as to think she will obey him. How dare he try and spoil her World Cup! By the time of the toss, she is so worked up that, on winning, contrary to the advice of her own coach and vice-captain, just to spite Saleem Euro, she decides to bat first, instead of putting South Africa in.

Her decision is met with bewilderment when she returns to the dressing room.

'Sanam, why did you do that, when we discussed this? There's moisture in the pitch and it's still overcast. The ball will swing and seam. If we sent them in to bat first, we could have knocked them over cheaply, all the while protecting our batters from the conditions. What have you done?'

'It's fine Fatima. Don't overthink it. We'll still win this match. We'll win because we're the better team. And as for conditions, well, these are the conditions we'll have to play in throughout the tournament. Better to get used to them early than later.'

But Fatima's apprehensions are proved correct in Pakistan's innings. With such heavy cloud cover, the South African opening bowlers, their captain Sabine Machheimer and the tall seamer Anna Mathewson swing the ball like a banana and wreak havoc. Nadia Malik and Ayesha Mufti are soon back in the pavilion, with the score still on nought. Fatima resists for a while, not really attempting to score, so much as just stay at the wicket. But a perfect leg cutter from Mathewson accounts for her, and after that, the batting order becomes a procession, no one staying in very long. In fact the only one who cannot really blame the conditions for her dismissal is Sanam. With the circumstances of the match furthering her frustration and anger, she tries to hit her way out of trouble. The first two balls she faces are dispatched for fours, but she hits the third one in the air, and is safely caught. Sanam is so furious that on her return to the dressing room, she throws her bat through a window. Some late blows from Sassui give the score a modicum of respectability, but the innings still ends with South Africa needing only 91 to win.

Sanam kicks herself for her stupidity at the toss. She made an impetuous decision as a result of her anger and outrage at Saleem Euro's brazen offer. And now, because of her, the team faces defeat.

The South African innings begins early, since Pakistan did not even bat out their full quota of overs. As if to add insult to injury, the sun breaks through just as the pair of smiling South African openers walk out to the wicket. The commentators on TV are unanimous in their opinion that the error of judgement shown by the Pakistan captain at the toss has already cost her team the match. That's the last thing Sanam hears as she leads her team out. She swears to herself that she will prove them all wrong.

In all their warm up games, it has been Farzana, the sturdy medium pacer, who has bowled the first over. But as she marks her run-up, Sanam takes the ball from her hand without a word and starts walking towards the start of her own run-up. Her first ball is brutish, and raps Machheimer, the South African captain, on her knuckles, causing her to drop her bat. There is a delay while the physio comes on to treat the bruised knuckle with cold spray. The next ball is more of the same though, an even shorter delivery aimed at Machheimer's head, which she only just manages to top edge for six behind the keeper. The blond South African girl turns and glares at Sanam reproachfully, as if trying to knock her head off the ball after her knuckles got bruised, is not the done thing in polite society. But this is not polite society, this is war. And Sanam, contrary to what many of her teammates are probably thinking, is no longer lashing out emotionally, but deliberately bowling this way as part of a tactic. This becomes evident on the next ball, which is slow and low, and shatters Machheimer's stumps.

Over the next four overs of her spell, Sanam bowls better than she has probably ever bowled in her life. It isn't just her intimidating pace, or her unerring accuracy, or the uncomfortable angles she creates when bowling short pitched balls to the batsmen. The spell is a combination of all these attributes, a testament to her mastery of her craft. Mumford is unable to cover Sanam's left-handed angle and edges to Fatima; Tsotsole is knocked off her feet by a toe-crushing Yorker, ending up lying in the dirt as her stumps disintegrate; Henderson and Harrison are both bounced out, trying to fend off the balls whose trajectory is aimed at their throats; and Kohler pops the one slower ball in the spell back to Sanam for a simple catch. By the time Sanam is finished with her spell, so are South Africa. With Farzana chipping in with a useful wicket at the other end, the Springbok girls are 36 for 7 after just eight overs.

Sanam, who has bowled at full pace, giving no further thought to trying to bowl within herself to protect her injury, is in acute pain by the time she delivers her last ball. Her side muscles feel like they're on fire, and only the sheer adrenaline generated by the match situation allows her to finish her spell. She is in so much pain she can barely stand, and so she has to seek treatment off the field. But by this time, the rest of the match is a formality. South Africa stumble through the remainder of the innings like shell shocked survivors of an artillery barrage. Fatima captains competently in Sanam's absence and Sassui bamboozles the remaining batsmen to hand Pakistan a quite unexpected 42 run victory.

Still wincing from the pain, Sanam remains on the treatment table and does not join her teammates' loud celebrations as they return to the dressing room. Sensing that the captain is still angry at something, the other girls keep their distance from Sanam. Only Fatima approaches her, and hands her the match ball as a souvenir. 'Well done captain. I'm sorry, I shouldn't have doubted you.'

CHAPTER 8

The Park Lane Hilton in London is normally a sedate place, a luxurious oasis, surrounded by the hustle and bustle of Mayfair on one side and the verdant green pastures of Hyde Park on the other. The lobby, with its gleaming marble floors, highly polished oak reception desk and expensive floral arrangements, is meant to calm the hotel's patrons from the moment they walk in. The demeanour of the ever-friendly staff, who always seem to remember sir or madam from a previous visit, even if sir or madam have stepped into the hotel for the first time in their lives, is also meant to further put the hotel's wealthy and well-heeled guests at ease.

However, the onset of the World Cup has seen the hordes of the cricket world descend upon the Hilton, irrevocably shattering its tranquillity. Five of the teams, India, Pakistan, Sri Lanka, England and South Africa, have been housed here along with their legions of support staff and numerous other board and cricket council officials. This concentration has therefore turned the hotel lobby into the central axis of the cricketing world for the next four weeks. At any given time you can find track-suited young women being marched by their minders to or from practice or matches. Legendary West Indian fast bowlers confer with potbellied Indian media moguls about the future of the game while sipping double espressos and munching on Macaroons in the foyer coffee shop. Photographers, cameramen, and journalists hunt in packs like Velociraptors, laying ambushes in the hope of cornering a player or official before they can reach the safety of the elevator bank. And fans of all shapes and sizes loiter in the lobby, hoping to catch a selfie with their idols.

The return of the Pakistan team, after their Lazarus-like victory over South Africa, is a particularly raucous one. The girls are greeted by an outbreak of spontaneous applause as they walk in, and then several green-shirted fans, who had been pretending to show genuine interest in purchasing a De Beers diamond from the in-house jewellery store, start up a chorus of 'Pakistan Zindabad', startling the jewel-laden saleslady.

Sanam smiles wanly, her sides still hurting, and signs a few obligatory autographs. Among the throngs of genuine fans, she spots an irate-looking Saleem Euro, still accompanied by his male model companion from the previous night. Only now, the boybander, like Euro, has a malevolent pout on his face. Euro pushes his way towards her, looking more and more ticked off with every push and shove he gets from the other fans.

'What you did? What you did Sanam? What the Haill! I told you, put South Afreeka in to bat after toss. That was where the odds were. Why you made such silly decision to bat first? This arrangement doesn't work this way. When we make deal, you have to follow through! Otherwise you there are conseequainces. Dan-gerus conseequainces.'

Sanam's temper, which has been simmering all day long, just snaps. 'You listen to me, I didn't make any goddamn deal with you. I don't work for you! You don't own me! Why don't you just get the fuck out of here!'

Sanam's raised voice and use of English swear words shocks not only Saleem Euro, but draws startled glances from both the security guard standing next to her trying to keep the crowds back, and from Fatima, who is also standing within earshot. The two girls get into an elevator together, but Fatima, despite her shocked expression, holds her tongue in the presence of the half dozen other passengers in the elevator. Its only when the two girls exit on their floor that Fatima grabs Sanam's shoulder.

'Captain, what the hell was that?'

'It's…It's nothing Fatima.'

'It's something! Who is that man? Have you been talking to bookies?'

'No! Of course not! I…that man was Saleem Euro. He came to my room last night, talked a lot of rubbish about wanting to help the team with anything they needed. And then, as he left, he said I should put South Africa in to bat if I won the toss.'

'Did he offer you money for this?'

'No. Yes. I…he didn't make an overt gesture, but he suggested that he wanted to have the same kind of relationship with me as he had with Babar sir in his playing days.'

'Sanam, I told you not to let these people into our team. I told you not to trust Babar sir. He knew what Saleem Euro was going to offer you, that's why he told you to meet him. That *kanjar* will probably get a commission for introducing you to Euro. This will destroy us.'

'I know that! Why do you think I've been so angry all day? Why do you think I deliberately batted first, even though I knew the conditions in the first innings would be tough? I risked us losing the match because I didn't want this bastard to believe, even for a second, that I had done his bidding.'

'Ok. Ok, good thinking. But what do we do now? Have you told anyone?'

'No. All of this happened late last night, so there hasn't been time. I suppose I should report it to our coach.'

'No. Don't do that. Look, if you tell anyone about this, it will create a scandal for the team, even though we haven't done anything wrong. It will be a distraction from the tournament, because everyone, our girls, the other teams, the media, the board and the cricket council, will get caught up in this and we won't be able to focus on anything else. If you haven't told anyone else, and you didn't take any money from Euro, and you also didn't do what he told you to do, then we can walk away from this one quietly.'

'You really think I shouldn't tell anyone?'

'Look Sanam, you and I both know this is our chance to win the World Cup. Maybe the only chance we'll ever get. That Johnny Cochrane fellow told us how much we could expect to earn in endorsements, if we win. If you tell the authorities, you put all of that at risk. The council will take this seriously, and will start investigating us, even though we have nothing to hide. If it had been any other country, they wouldn't have taken it so seriously, but because it's Pakistan, with all the men's history of match-fixing, they'll definitely come after us. And at the end of the day, they'll find nothing, but it will ensure that this World Cup slips out of our fingers. Now I know you might not have the need for the money because your father is a rich factory owner, but I could certainly do with the kind of money Cochrane promised us. Just go to your room and forget about it.'

'But what if Euro comes back?'

'After the way you handled him downstairs, I doubt he'll come back. Your outburst may have worked in our favour. He would have spoken with Babar sir, Babar sir would also have told him that he was unlikely to have any luck with us, and he'll probably move on to some other team. So I don't think we have anything to worry about. Unless you report it. And don't forget, if you do report it, you'll have to tell the authorities how Saleem Euro contacted you. You'll have to tell them about Babar sir's involvement. And that would be the end of his career in the board. The evidence against him would be so much, after the earlier inquiries, he would be lucky to stay out of prison. But that would be the end of his reputation. He'd never coach again, anywhere in the world. His family would find out the truth; he's probably been lying to them for years, just as he's been lying to us. It would shatter him. So before you act like a goody-two-shoes, remember that. You'll ruin our chances, and you'll destroy him.'

*

The knock on her door brings Sanam out of the trance-like state she has been in for the past hour. Lying in front of her is the big orange box, now torn to shreds, with the beautiful Hermes bag also ripped and in pieces. The biggest reminder of Saleem Euro's visit. When she entered her room and saw it lying there, it became the target of her ire. After she had poured out her frustrations on it with a knife, she finally decided to take the risk of calling Him. She doesn't know if she can trust him, but she knows she has to talk to someone. And under the circumstances, he is perhaps one of the few people in the world right now who can truly understand what she is feeling.

'Sorry it took me so long, but I was stuck in this "Legends of Yesteryear" dinner that was being covered on TV, and to leave suddenly would have raised a lot of questions. So, looks like you've been having a party?'

Sanam lets FQ into her room, not failing to notice how good he looks in a tuxedo, with the black bow tie undone. A sort of Pakistani Cary Grant. She follows his gaze to the mess on her floor. 'I've got a problem.'

'Yeah, you said that on the phone. I assumed it was something to do with failing a drug test, or having a lover die in your room. Whenever I got one of those calls from my teammates in the past, those were the kind of problems they had when they said it was an emergency. I'm not sure getting your designer bag fixed falls in the same category. Unless you've hidden the dead lover in the cupboard.'

His attempt at levity finally brings a smile to her face for the first time in 24 hours. 'I haven't called you to get my bag fixed. And there's no lover in the cupboard. I called you because…' Sanam takes a deep breath and decides to take the plunge. She will have to trust someone. So she relates the whole Saleem Euro episode to him, and also relates to him Fatima's advice.

He listens to the entire story and doesn't ask any questions. She looks into his eyes to see if there is any hint of judgement or disapproval of her, but she spots nothing. He is totally understanding. Finally, he picks up the ripped Hermes bag and starts shoving it back into the orange box.

'What are you doing?'

'I'm doing the obvious. Getting rid of this bag. It's the only thing that links you with Saleem Euro. Tearing it into pieces won't solve anything. Put on something more formal than a tracksuit and come with me.'

He holds the orange box as they walk through the lobby of the hotel and hail a taxi. She has quickly put on a pair of jeans and a top, and anyone watching would assume that the pair of them was going out for nothing more devious than a late coffee. She is nervous and her eyes keep trailing to the orange box, but she tries to hide her anxiety. FQ on the other hand, is nonchalant, totally unfazed, as if destroying evidence is something he does on a daily basis.

It's only when they are in the taxi that she finally speaks. 'Where are we going?'

'Bar Boulud. It's a place I know, in the Mandarin Oriental hotel.'

'Why are we going there?'

'Why? Because the chef there does this great brisket slider, with Russian mayonnaise and swiss cheese, and I couldn't eat the crap they served at the Legends dinner.'

'What? But what about the…'

FQ puts a finger to his lips and smiles benevolently, as if trying to explain something to a small child. 'And I figure that you are so stressed out, you need to chill out, otherwise you'll never be able to play in this tournament. Plus, there is a huge dumpster at the side of the hotel, where we can throw away your bag. Pity though, it was a very nice bag. Just the sort my ex-wife would have loved.'

The taxi drops them off in front of the Mandarin Oriental hotel in Knightsbridge. FQ gets off, and in one graceful motion tosses the box into the dumpster, before taking Sanam's hand and leading her into the restaurant. Bar Bouloud is a watering hole for the rich and famous. Even at this late hour, it is packed. Investment bankers in striped shirts and suspenders order £400 bottles of Cristal champagne as if they were ordering tap water. Footballers and their glamour model girlfriends inhabit cosy corner tables and share intimate suppers. Minor celebrities jostle each other for a place at the bar, trying to impress the gorgeous, Amazonian maître d' into giving them a table. They are stunned when, having given them all short shrift, she greets FQ by name, and immediately leads Sanam and him to a corner booth.

'A bottle of champagne, and some fresh strawberries Katya. And can you ask Pierre to do some of his delicious sliders as well?'

'Of course Mr. Qureshi.' The maître d' leans low, and the open top buttons on her shirt allow both of them to get an ample view of her bosom.

'Well she was being *overly* friendly.' Sanam's tone reveals an edge of annoyance.

FQ grins goofily. 'Why, are you jealous?'

'No, not at all. Why would I be jealous? And why did you order a drink for me? I don't drink.'

'Trust me, if anyone needs a drink, you do, after what you've been through in the last 24 hours. Relax, it's just a little champagne, and besides, you don't have a game tomorrow. You need to learn to unwind Sanam.'

A waitress brings their drinks to the table. Sanam feels a quiver of excitement as FQ's arm brushes against hers in the cramped booth. She has never been a fan of drinking, but at his urging, takes a sip from the flute. It isn't bad, less bitter than she expected, with a fruity tinge.

'So, how come you've never drunk before? You were in university here in England, weren't you? Or is it a religious thing?'

'It's not a religious thing. My father drinks. Quite a bit, actually. But I never wanted to do it. I don't like losing control.'

'A control freak, huh? Fair enough. I also notice you don't like letting your guard down. But sometimes it's a good thing to do both. Here, try it with a strawberry. It'll bring out the flavour. Cheers.'

He clinks his flute with hers and she takes another sip after biting on the strawberry. He is right, it does bring out the flavour more. The champagne is beginning to grow on her.

'So when did you start drinking?'

'Me? The first tour I went on. I was barely 18. Skipper was injured and we were in New Zealand. Kashif *paaji* was the senior bowler and the vice-captain. We used to call him *paaji* because he had been around for ages. I think he played his first test in the late '60s or something. He was a brilliant bowler. Very limited in his talent, but his experience and knowledge of what to do with a ball was just out of this world. Only problem was, he didn't want to share any of his wisdom with a junior bowler like me, because he viewed me as a threat to his place in the side. So he called me to his room the night before the first test. I had just been informed by the captain that I would be playing in the morning and I was buzzing with excitement. And here, all of a sudden, after having ignored me completely up till that point, *Paaji* was now acting so friendly and giving me so much lift. So I go to his room eager to soak up whatever wisdom he imparts, and he's sitting there, with a bottle of scotch and two glasses. He hands me a glass and tells me to drink. He tells me that drinking copious amounts of scotch the night before a test was the secret behind his longevity. He gave me some bullshit about how the alcohol kept the joints lubricated and took the edge of your nerves. I was a stupid kid, so I believed him and drank a glass. And then another. And another. By the time I left his room, I was completely shitfaced. He was so insecure about losing his place to me, that he wanted to get me drunk so I would screw up the next day and hopefully get dropped for the next match.'

'What a jerk! So then what happened?'

'I woke up feeling horrible, barely got to the ground. Babar, who was the keeper, saw I was in a pretty lousy state, and on top of that, we lost the toss and had to field first. I begged Babar not to tell the captain, so he had me drink three cups of black coffee. It was vile. But it enabled me to get out onto the pitch and the captain brought me in first change. From the first over, my rhythm felt good and the more I bowled, the better I felt. I ended up taking ten wickets in the match. *Paaji* never invited me for a drink ever again, I can tell you that!'

'So tell me, why did you not throw the bag in the dumpster near our hotel? Why here?'

'Because the media is all over our hotel. You don't know what lengths journalists will go to, to get a juicy story at a tournament like this. I've been on tours where members of the press were literally going through our trash. That's why I figured it was better to get rid of any 'evidence' away from the scene of the crime. Plus, like I said, the Slider here is actually out of this world.'

'God, it sounds so awful when you talk about it like that. Evidence, scene of the crime. I don't know how I let myself get stuck in this mess. I don't know why I let that asshole into my room.'

'You did it because he invoked Babar's name. It's as simple as that. He knew you would never be able to refuse him entry if he mentioned his relationship with Babar. It happens. I blame Babar. He knew what Saleem Euro was going to ask of you. He should have protected you.'

'All those years, I always believed it when Babar sir said he was innocent. But now, I just don't know what to believe. Do you think Babar sir was fixing matches for this Saleem Euro?'

FQ takes a bite out of his burger and contemplates his glass. 'Babar did some silly things over the years. He was always a little too fond of money. I'm not saying there's anything wrong with that. I like money too. But Babar always wanted to hustle some extra on the side. He'd put down side bets on how many runs he'd score or catches he would take. He did it with us, so it wouldn't have been very difficult to graduate to bookies. They were always there. Always around the hotels, the grounds, in airports. They would always try to speak to the players, introducing themselves as a friend of a friend, or something similar. Nothing obvious, very low key. The first time I started really noticing their presence was on the West Indies tour six months before the World Cup. That was incidentally, also the first time I found out that there was such a thing as match-fixing.'

'Did someone approach you?'

'Not exactly. I remember, we were in Trinidad, near the end of the tour. We had been away from home for about three months. Three months in the Caribbean may sound idyllic, but trust me, when you are hopping from one lousy island to the next every few days, and eating the same shitty jerk chicken with rice and beans at the ground every day, you get sick of it. We had already won the test series and we were leading 3-1 in the one-dayers. We had one match left, and we were happy to be in Trinidad because it meant the tour was almost finished. A local South Asian businessman had invited us to his house for dinner and we were all keen to go because we hadn't had a good home-cooked desi meal for weeks. The businessman's wife had cooked this massive vat of goat curry and Babar and I were on our third helping, when Ajju came over. He said a friend of his had told him the funniest thing, that there could be good money on offer if we lost the last match. I was so naïve, I asked him how we would make money if we lost, since the Board would only give us our bonuses if we won. Ajju said the money wasn't from the board, it was from private individuals. They were willing to pay a bunch of us to lose the game. Babar immediately asked how much. Ajju said he wasn't sure, but it could be close to fifty thousand dollars. I said it was funny that we were being offered more to lose the game than we were paid to win it. The others laughed and no one thought any more of it, but Babar kept pushing Ajju to go talk to his friend and to try and get more money. I forgot the whole incident, but the next morning, when we got to the ground, all hell broke loose. Somehow, Skipper had found out, and he was pissed. He shut the dressing room door so that even the team support staff weren't allowed in, and then he ripped into us. He took out a copy of the Quran and made all of us swear that we weren't going to throw the game. He said if he suspected, even for an instant, that someone hadn't performed to the best of their abilities, that player would never play under him again. That scared the shit out of all of us. I think we ended up winning the game by about a hundred runs. Everyone took wickets, everyone got runs, no one wanted Skipper to doubt them. I think the only one who got out cheaply was Ajju, but he got a genuinely unplayable ball from Mikey Gilchrist.'

'So did Skipper throw anyone out of the team?'

'Well, a few days later, he came to me and asked me whether I thought Ajju was involved with bookies. Like I said, I didn't know what a bookie was at that time, so I told him I didn't think so, and that Ajju had most probably told the story at dinner as a joke. The concept of someone willing to pay us fifty thousand dollars to lose, was just alien to me. Skipper just grunted and didn't say anything else, but our next home series against India, we found out that Ajju had been dropped due to bad form, even though he had done quite well in the West Indies. I saw that team sheet and thanked God I hadn't responded in any way to Ajju's offer.'

'Wow. But then you said they came back? The bookies I mean. Skipper wasn't able to keep them out?'

'Well, they started showing up a lot more after Skipper retired. They were petrified of being caught by Skipper. But after he left, they became bolder.'

'But after Skipper retired, you became captain. If you knew, couldn't you have stopped them?'

'I wish I had, in hindsight. But I didn't know how. At the time, I was a very young captain, barely 23 or 24. All the other guys were senior to me. Some of them had known these bookies socially for years. Any time I tried to restrict who could and couldn't meet members of the team, the guys got angry, said I was trying to throw my weight around because the captaincy had gone to my head. I was just so anxious to do well, I didn't want to start feuds within the team. So I tolerated their presence. I tolerated people like Babar and Ajju having a chat with them once a while, giving out some titbits about team selection and little things like that. But I drew the line at match-fixing. I told them that any team led by me would never throw a game. And under my captaincy, nobody ever did. Whether we won or lost, we did it on our own.'

'Couldn't the board have helped you?'

'Ha. The board only helps those who can help themselves. Otherwise, they don't want you to tell them anything that might rock their gravy train. When Skipper was around, he ruled with an iron fist. No one dared to oppose him, and the board would jump through hoops to get him anything he wanted. He could do that. I couldn't. You see, I didn't go to Aitchison and Cambridge, and I didn't have an uncle who was a General in the martial-law government like he did. I came from an average middle-class home, and so the board felt it could push me around. Many of the bookies on the other hand, were very well connected. I remember, once I asked our team manager to ensure that no one used their mobile phones during a match. It was an important game, and I didn't want any distractions. Within half an hour, the board president came down and told me a federal minister was threatening to have me investigated if I didn't rescind the ban on the use of mobile phones. Apparently, a few of the bookies were trying to get through to get some team details, but no one was picking up. So they called the minister to help them out. This would never have happened with Skipper. He had connections. The only thing I had was my skill as a cricketer.'

Sanam is quiet for a moment as she sips her champagne, now enjoying the feel of the cool bubbles tickling her throat. 'FQ, Fatima says I shouldn't say anything to the authorities. About Saleem Euro. She says we will be the ones who are investigated and no good will come of it. What do you think?'

'I think Fatima is a smart girl. Look, you haven't done anything wrong. You didn't take money, you didn't take any kind of gift, and you didn't do what Saleem asked you to do.

You raise a flag over this, and this tournament will become all about match-fixing, rather than being about the beautiful Sanam Khan and her team of champions.'

He puts his hand on hers as he says the last sentence, gently stroking her fingers with his own. The feel of his skin is electrifying. Perhaps it's the alcohol in her bloodstream, but Sanam thinks FQ has never looked so handsome as he does now. Unconsciously, she leans toward him. His lips meet hers halfway, and suddenly Sanam is aware that she is doing something she has secretly dreamed of doing for the past fifteen years.

CHAPTER 9

T20 World Cup Group C Lord's Cricket Ground 3 June: PAK Women V WI Women: Pak W 178-4(Fatima Shah 86*, Ayesha Mufti 67) beat WI W 123 All Out (E Baptiste 25 Sassui Memon 5-21) by 55 runs.

The pain is excruciating. It rises from her side and spreads across her lower back, making it impossible for her to continue sleeping. Sanam knows, with all her experience of injuries, that this is a bad one. She keeps lying in bed, hoping for the pain to subside. Finally, after five minutes, she gingerly raises herself out of bed. Even that simplest of actions is jarring to her body. She reaches for the bottle of pain killers on the side table and pops a couple of pills. They are remarkably effective, and kick in within minutes, allowing her to walk to the bathroom. FQ got her these medicines discreetly, to avoid alerting and panicking the team physio. He has also arranged a couple of sessions for her with his old physio, to work on her injury. And indeed, Sanam had thought after those sessions that she was getting better, till this morning, when the pain returned, worse than ever before.

The thought of FQ brings a smile to her face. He has done so much for her this past week, providing her succour when she really needed it. He has been there for her in every way possible.

Most importantly, he has been *there,* talking to her, holding her, kissing her. Doing all the things that a boyfriend would do.

Boyfriend. That sounds like such a childish term. As if she was still sixteen. Sixteen-year-old girls have boyfriends. Thirty-two-year olds have, well...what? Lovers? Partners? Intendeds? In truth, she doesn't know how to label her relationship with FQ. She doesn't even know if it requires a label yet. After all, it's only been a week. But all she knows is that in this past week, she has felt things that she has never felt before.

Sanam had given up on finding romance in her life a while ago. She accepted it as one of the sacrifices she would have to make for her cricket. With her various touring and playing commitments, it would always have been difficult to find someone. And on top of the logistical issues, it would have been even harder to find a man, especially a Pakistani man, whose ego would be able to withstand dating a prominent, outspoken sportswoman. No small challenge then.

It wasn't as if Sanam had lived the life of a nun. She had had several relationships in university, but they were all fleeting college romances, never intended or likely to go anywhere. And since then, cricket, and the team, have been the only loves in her life. Thus she had reconciled herself to not ever really being in that position, of falling in love, or choosing a partner. In her mind, she had been ready to acquiesce to her mother's choice after her career ended. That was the unspoken agreement. Her life was her own until she retired from cricket. After that, she didn't really care what happened. And so the FQ situation is totally unprecedented for her. It is a school girl fantasy come to life. Only problem is, her fantasies never told her how the story ends.

It doesn't matter yet, she tells herself. She's still got a World Cup to get through. If she can get past this pain first. FQ will still be there on the 21st of June, when this tournament ends.

There's no rush to figure things out. Besides, no one knows about them, so there's nothing to worry about yet.

The ringing of the room phone brings her back to reality. She thinks about ignoring it altogether. Babar sir has been calling her for the past two days and she has refused to answer his calls. It must be him again, trying to give some kind of explanation for Saleem Euro. An explanation she doesn't want to hear. But the shrill, siren-like ring continues, and then it occurs to her that it might be Him. The thought of hearing his voice warms her and makes her cheeks flush. Sanam makes a mental note that she really must stop acting like a school girl when it comes to FQ, even as she limps toward the phone, and almost jumps the last yard to grab it before he hangs up.

'Hi F…'

'You could have at least given us the courtesy of some advance notice.' Her mother's voice is as overbearing as ever.

'Ma? Given you notice of what?'

'Of your gallivanting and doing God knows what else with that fellow. It's really so embarrassing to learn about my own daughter's escapades from the guests at your sister's engagement. I was absolutely mortified. Can you do nothing right for this family?'

'Ma, I have no idea what you're talking about, but can you please just calm down. I'm feeling quite sore today, I'm really not in the mood to take one of your ritual scoldings, if you don't mind.'

'Hmph. Suit yourself. Be evasive. But this time, it's not just me that's concerned. Your father couldn't sleep last night, after he heard the news. I know you constantly ignore anything I say, perhaps you'll listen to him. And one last thing before I hand your father the phone. At least get a promise from that fellow to marry you, before you allow him into your pants. He may not be the ideal match, but beggars can't be choosers.'

'Maa!!!' Sanam shouts down the phone, but her mother's voice is replaced by the softer, gentler tone of her father.

'*Beta* Sanam, are you there? This is Baba Jan.'

'Baba Jan, what is Ma talking about? I have no clue.'

'Beta, a story broke in the media yesterday. We were so busy in the arrangements for your sister's engagement, we didn't notice till some of the guests mentioned it to us. It's a story about you…you and…Faisal Qureshi….you were seen together…doing something…'

Sanam's mouth becomes dry and her heart feels like it is about to explode out of her chest, as she finally understands what her father is saying. How could the story of her relationship with FQ have gotten out so fast? No one knows about it, even in her team.

'Baba…I…Uh…'

'Beta, I can't hear you. It's not true is it? I've told your mother it cannot be true. I told her Sanam has never done anything remotely like this. And she certainly wouldn't indulge…in anything…with *that* scoundrel…. after all he did…you wouldn't, would you?'

'Baba Jan…I…'

There is silence on the other end of the line as the implication of her hesitation begins to sink in.

'Oh. I…see. Look Sanam, you know I am not like your mother. I have never wanted to force anyone upon you. I was always confident that whomever you chose, romantically, you would make a sound choice because I have implicit trust in your judgement. Now, I don't know exactly what's going on over there, and I understand it's a very high-pressure environment due to the World Cup. But I would just ask you to consider this. This man…lied to his country. He betrayed his country. He betrayed his family. Most importantly, he betrayed the game that you and I both love. He cannot be right for you.'

'Baba…it's not like that. FQ has just helped me with my injuries. It's nothing more…'

'Look beta, if you tell me that, I will believe you. But perception is everything, and the perception seems to be that there is a lot more going on. I just want to say…be very careful. This man doesn't deserve you and he cannot be trusted.'

Her father hangs up, and Sanam feels as if she is having a stroke. She has never lied to her father like that. She doesn't know why she did it right now, what compelled her to deny whatever it is she has with FQ. She tells herself it's just the shock of being ambushed like that by her mother, nothing else. It's not like she feels somehow guilty, for getting pleasure in the company of FQ. But she still cannot for the life of her figure out how the news has spread so quickly to Pakistan.

And then she opens her hotel door and understands. Piled on her doorstep are the morning editions of London's leading tabloids. Each of them has a picture of her, leaving Bar Boloud with FQ, holding his hand and intimately nuzzling his ear. Ever since that night, a week ago, they have been returning every evening to Bar Boloud. It has become their place, where they can be intimate with each other. Their mistake, for assuming someone wouldn't notice a pattern. And in a World Cup that has so far been free from controversies, the news of a romance between the attractive captain of the Pakistan team and a retired superstar of the game, is just too good a story for the press to miss.

Sanam spends the next two hours giving explanations to the team management about what is quickly labelled 'the FQ situation'. Each discussion with a team official, where she is obliged to repeat the story she gave her father, makes her temper rise a little more. She feels like a suspect in a murder investigation, having to provide alibis to refute the press claims. Why should she have to put up with this, when her only crime is to have spent a little time with a man she is attracted to. It's not even as if they released a sex tape. Just a little hand-holding and canoodling. But she is subjected to an interrogation that would have made the Grand Inquisitor Torquemada proud. She wishes FQ would call, as speaking to him is the only thing that will calm her down. But then she remembers that he is off on a golf trip in Scotland with some old county colleagues this weekend.

All of this is hardly the ideal preparation for today's game, even if she were fully fit. By the time she finally finishes her meeting with the media manager, the team has already left for the ground, and Sanam's brain is too fried to be able to concentrate on cricket. She reaches Lord's and informs the team that she isn't fit enough to play. No questions are asked, as everyone is aware of Sanam's situation. Besides, Fatima is there to fill in for her, and the opposition, the West Indies women's team, is coming off a 12-match losing streak and are not expected to give the Pakistanis a difficult time. Having made her announcement, Sanam exits the dressing room as quickly as possible. She doesn't want to spend the day sitting with her team mates in the pavilion, in the full glare of the press contingent.

Luckily a refuge is close at hand. Mick, the Middlesex physio who has been treating her on FQ's recommendation, has a small treatment room at the ground, and so she lies down on his table and allows him to work on her back while she follows the game on a small TV screen. She feels a pang of guilt for having dropped out of the match. Pulling out of a match because of a personal situation is something that she has never done before, and certainly something she never thought she would do in a World Cup. It goes against every principle she has, and it's something she has berated other players for in the past. But between her mental state and the pain in her body, it is simply too much for her. She would have felt worse had the team been troubled, but Fatima and the girls put on a thoroughly professional display, not allowing Sanam's absence to be felt.